L IKE HER UNCLE'S HOUSE, MARK'S SAT UP OFF THE ground, giving way to low thatches of grass. All Lindsay had to do was cling to the side of the house and step on those. Sure she would still leave prints, but they wouldn't be nearly as obvious as tromping through the sand. She moved fast but carefully from one tuft of grass to the next.

At Mark's window, she peered in. He stood on the other side of the small desk, looking absolutely miserable. His eyes were swollen as if he'd been crying. Dark circles painted the puffy skin beneath. He looked very thin and quite ill.

Lindsay put her palms against the glass and pulled, but it didn't budge. Inside, Mark shook his head.

"They locked it," he called.

WICKED DEAD

SNARED

BY
STEFAN PETRUCHA
AND THOMAS PENDLETON

HARPER TEEN

AN IMPRINT OF HARPERCOLLINSPUBLISHERS

Grateful acknowledgment is given to Shaun O'Boyle
for the use of the title page image, © Shaun O'Boyle.
More of his evocative photographs can be seen on
www.oboylephoto.com.

HarperTeen is an imprint of
HarperCollins Publishers.

Library of Congress Cataloging-in-Publication Data
Petrucha, Stefan.
  Snared / by Stefan Petrucha and Thomas Pendleton. —
1st HarperTeen paperback ed.
    p. cm. — (Wicked dead)
  Summary: Sixteen-year-old Lindsay is disgusted at the
prospect of a beach trip with her parents, but her vaca-
tion gets interesting—and dangerous—when she meets
Mark, the boy next door.
  ISBN 978-0-06-113851-5 (pbk.)
    [1. Devil—Fiction. 2. Supernatural—Fiction. 3.
Vacations—Fiction. 4. Beaches—Fiction. 5. Horror sto-
ries.] I. Pendleton, Thomas, date II. Title.
PZ7.P44727Sn 2007   2007010888
[Fic]—dc22   CIP
                                                   AC

Typography by Christopher Stengel
❖
First Edition, 2008

THOMAS PENDLETON DEDICATES THIS BOOK TO
J. C. P. AND NICHOLAS KAUFMANN,
A COUPLE OF THE WICKED ONES.

STEFAN PETRUCHA DEDICATES THIS BOOK TO THE
DEAD—MARTIN, FELICIA, AMELIA, MICHAEL, FRANK,
MARY, JOSEPH L., AND THE MANY OTHERS HE
DOES NOT KNOW. HE HOPES YOU'VE ALL GOT A
GREAT GAME GOING SOMEWHERE.

PROLOGUE

A gaping wound the size of a dead body sat in a corner of Lockwood Orphanage's once-fine copper roof, exposing the Headmistress's quarters to the elements. Over years, rain and snow had seeped between brick and mortar while hungry moss and lichen patiently worked downward to reclaim the plaster walls and wooden supports. Like an animal, rot crawled into all the cracks, then grew and pushed to make more room for itself. Here the lines between civilization and nature, chaos and order, were severed. Here everything knew that one day, the whole of the old Georgian mansion would be gone.

A few stories down, though fragile, the precious

lines remained: The hallway that ran the length of the building was relatively dry, its curved roof marked at regular intervals by fixtures that seemed as if they might light up; bulletin boards still bore dusty papers announcing meetings, tests, and plays. Here the mansion seemed intent to go on forever, as if it were yet the host of living things.

And the ghosts of the place could not help but play along.

Three figures, whose presence disturbed not even the air, moved as one along the narrow wooden floor. On one side of the hall, there was only darkness from the open doors, but on the other, the pale moon cast oblong rectangles of light. As the trio walked, they wove in and out of the shadows.

Every so often the shortest, timid Shirley, would draw her woolen high-necked pajamas close around her shoulders. Her green eyes wide beneath her straight red hair, she'd peer deeply into one of the doorways. This went on, room after room, until finally, too nervous to keep silent any longer, she stopped dead in her tracks and called, "Anne!"

Her high-pitched voice echoed down the long hall.

"Not so loud!" Daphne, the tallest, warned.

Shirley tugged at her hair. "Sorry. I'm just . . . I mean . . . you don't suppose the Headmistress did something . . . permanent to her?"

Mary grimaced and shook her head, sending her blond curls swinging. "No. The Headmistress fancies herself our guardian. She believes her wicked punishments are for our own good. Anne must be off somewhere, licking her wounds after the Red Room."

The name sent a chill through Shirley, and the other girls briefly wondered if she might have another anxiety attack. Instead she settled herself and just asked, "What's it like, the Red Room?"

Before Mary could begin to conjure a description of the hellish place, Daphne's arms shot out, stopping her companions. As they stood silently for a second, they all distinctly heard the creak of a floorboard. Then it went still.

"That's not the Headmistress," Daphne whispered, raising an eyebrow. She lifted her voice. "Anne, will you come out? We looked for you until dawn last night and we've already been at it for hours tonight. We just want to make sure you're all right! Let us help you!"

Silence.

Daphne hissed. "She's a stubborn bee."

A slight smile came to Mary's lips. "I know something that might draw her out." A flash of lush vermilion appeared at the waist of her white nightgown. "A little honey for our reluctant bee."

Shirley was aghast. "You're taking out the Clutch right here? In the hall?"

Still smiling, Mary adjusted her gown and sat down in the center of the hall. "Yes. Why not? It's as good a place as any. There are plenty of exits in case we're disturbed." Then she placed the bag in her lap and started to unknot its golden cord.

Shirley couldn't believe it. It all seemed so wrong. Her heart spoke out loudly before her brain could quite catch up. "But we can't play without Anne again!"

At once realizing the consequences if Anne were listening, she clapped her hand to her mouth.

Pretending she hadn't heard Shirley's ill-timed admission, Mary upturned the vermilion silk sack as if she were a stage magician preparing a tantalizing trick. Five bones, copper-brown with age, spilled onto the floor.

Helter skelter they all rolled, this way and that, chattering into one another on their random way.

"Let's see if these catch her eye," Mary said as they spread along the uneven floor. Soon enough, all the bones came to a stop, except for one, the skull. It didn't seem to want to stop spinning. Long after it should have gone still, it continued to inch along the floor, as if pushed by a mouse, to the edge of a hole where it finally, just barely, came to a stop. Then, all on its own, it flipped up, jaw to the ceiling, as if taking a nap.

Perplexed, the three girls watched, until slowly the darkness above the skull shimmered as if the air were a pond disturbed by a stray wind. A pale white shape took form: a foot, its big toe pressing angrily down hard on the fragile bone.

Shirley spoke first. "Oh. Anne. Hi. Didn't realize you were there." Her voice rose an octave per word.

"No, kidding, Nancy Drool," Anne replied as she made the rest of herself more visible. Her long black hair and black T-shirt still left her half-hidden in shadow, but her eyes glowed with rage like twin moons in a starless sky. "Planning to play without me, huh?"

Daphne scrunched her face. "Don't be ridiculous. Of course not ... we'd never ..."

Anne raised her foot as if to crush the skull.

"Anne, do you mind?" Mary said, gasping. "I understand you're upset. I understand why, after the wretched experience you've been through, but should you slip, even by accident, you might ..."

Anne looked up with a wicked grin. "Bust it? Then what, Goldilocks? We'd all be like stuck here forever? Like we aren't already?"

"The bones are our chance. Our only way out of here," Daphne said plainly. "Yours, too."

"So you say," Anne snorted. "How do I know you're not lying just to mess with my head? Hey, I can't trust you to wait for me for a few lousy hours while I'm being tortured; why should I trust you on anything?" Surprisingly, her voice was choked with emotion. "I saved our asses big-time, and you all just abandon me to big Queen Freak-Shriek, and then you ... then you ..."

She shook her head and pushed down harder on the skull, rocking it roughly against the wooden floor.

"None of us can fight the Headmistress, you

6

know that," Daphne said. "And if we wanted to play without you, don't you think we would have by now?"

"Yeah, well, problem being, I know you already did," Anne said. "I saw you."

Daphne stiffened. Mary bolted to her feet, looking as if she might try to grab the skull. Shirley blurted out, "It was all Mary's idea!"

Mary turned to her, enraged. "It's not as though you voiced strong objection!"

Anne laughed bitterly. "Nice to see you turn on each other for a change. But I'm not buying."

She vanished again. At once the skull lurched forward and a crunch was heard.

The three watching girls winced and closed their eyes, but when they opened them again, the little skull was still intact.

Anne laughed long and hard as she reappeared. "Just cracking my knuckles."

Daphne stormed up to her. "Stop it, Anne. Stop it right now. Get your foot off that bone and sit down. You're upset, fine—who wouldn't be after the Red Room—but you know you wouldn't dare crush that bone on purpose! We've had enough stupid accidents after last night, haven't we?"

Shirley lowered her head at the reference to her own fit the night before. Her fingers rooted nervously through her hair. Anne wondered if the red-haired jitter-ball had finally realized it was her yowling that had brought the Headmistress in the first place.

Daphne continued. "We're in a bad spot, that's all. Things happen. I'm sorry about my part in it. Come back to earth and we'll all decide together what to do next."

Just then Shirley's fingers found what they were looking for. They yanked a strand of hair free from her skull. She hugged herself, seeming to take pleasure in the sharp, sudden pain. "Maybe Anne's urge isn't so crazy," she said quietly. "Maybe it's just who she is."

Daphne rolled her eyes. "Kid, you're not helping."

"No. Let *Kid* talk," Anne said. "I'd like to know what *Kid* thinks."

When Daphne fell silent, Shirley smiled nervously. "Well, it's just that right now you remind me of an old Russian folktale. God comes to a peasant and asks what she's praying for. 'My neighbor has a fine cow that gives great milk, and I have none,' she says. 'So,' God says, 'you want a cow like hers?'

'No,' the woman answers, 'I want her cow to die.' "

Shirley's eyes flashed, revealing a glimpse of the deeper darkness that throbbed beneath her skittish exterior. Anne snickered in appreciation.

"Anne," Mary said softly, "forget about us a moment. Don't you realize we've no notion of how the bones work or why? Crush it, and who knows what you might unleash? It could make the Headmistress and her Red Room seem like a fresh spring day."

"Like it could really be worse than the Red Room." Anne's face twitched at the memory.

Daphne's face softened. "You're right. We should've been there for you. But we're human. Or at least we were. The night was young; there was time for another story. With the Headmistress busy, we had to take the chance."

Mary turned to Anne. "Look in your heart. Can you honestly say you wouldn't have done the same?"

Anne scowled. "You bet your phantom-ass I would have. But if it'd been any of you locked up in there screaming, the other two wouldn't have let me."

Daphne met her eyes.

"You're right," she said evenly. "We're sorry."

Anne twisted her head to the side and smirked. "That and a dollar gets me a cup of coffee."

"You make it so difficult," Mary said. "We'd already planned to give you three turns in a row."

"Oh?"

"It's true," Shirley said, nodding. "Three turns. It was Daphne's idea."

"Tonight? Do I get these turns tonight?"

Daphne nodded at Anne, whose toe was still on the skull. "Deal?"

Anne lifted her toe and gave the bone a push. It rolled across the dusty floor, leaving a wormy trail. When it came near, Shirley bent over and snatched it. She cradled it in both hands, brought it close to her face, and smiled.

A funny look came over her as she regarded the bone. "Ever wonder what it looked like with the flesh on it? Sometimes I think I see little indentations in the brow, for horns."

"Enough girl talk," Anne said with a sneer as she plopped down on the floor. "I get three rolls. Hand them over."

"Fine," Shirley said. She sat down herself, scooped the other bones from the floor, and handed them all to Anne.

Anne took them at once and quickly rolled them. Nothing. Again. Nothing.

She grabbed them up in one hand and held them a moment, regarding them with distrust. The bones were cold in her hands. They didn't feel quite right. Something was off. Had the others done something to them?

I wouldn't put it past them.

Blasting cool air from her nostrils, she didn't even bother to shake the bones when she threw the third time. Something in her gut told her not to expect to win, and her expectations were fulfilled.

"Sorry. That's three turns. Deal's up. Mary told the last story, so it's my turn now," Daphne said.

"Thanks for not cheering," Anne muttered as she passed along the bones.

Daphne confidently went down onto her knees, shook the bones in one hand, then let them roll palm to floor, as if she were shooting craps. Despite points for style and bravado, she lost.

"Maybe the bones are angry because we were fighting," Shirley wondered aloud as she reached for them.

Anne leaned back on her haunches and gave

her a look. "Whatever. We should stop soon. It's late, the storm's long over, and it's easier for her to hear us."

Mary tsked. "If it's late, it's only because we spent so much time searching for you. No interest in taking any risks now that your three are up? How kind. How typical."

Anne held up three fingers to Mary. "Read between the lines."

Shirley cleared her throat. "It's a good thing," she said, rattling the bones in her cupped hands, "we're not fighting over a boy."

"A boy," Daphne mused, "would be easier to carve up."

Giggling, perhaps at the image of a carved boy, Shirley threw the bones. They spread on the floor in a tight pattern. The one that looked like a thigh-bone spun freely, so they couldn't quite tell what it was until it stopped.

When it did, Anne put her hands behind her back, and clenched them both into fists. The three symbols had come up.

"We have a winner," Daphne said.

But Shirley didn't look like a winner. One second, she looked confused. The next, her body stiffened as if she were having a seizure. She moaned, raising her shoulders.

"What is it?" Mary said.

Anne's eyes narrowed. Usually whoever rolled the winning pattern felt a little light-headed as the story came to her, but this wasn't that.

"No," Shirley said, shaking her head faster and faster. "I won't say it. I won't."

She clenched her teeth and pushed air between them. Her hissing mixed with spittle.

Daphne looked concerned. "Shirley, what's going on?"

"Maybe she'll explode," Anne suggested wryly.

"Quiet! She's fighting the story. She's trying not to tell it," Mary said.

"Can you do that?" Anne asked, genuinely curious.

"I don't know," Mary responded.

"From the looks of her, I'm guessing no," Daphne said. "Shirley, stop! Don't fight it!"

"No, I won't say it. I won't. . . ."

Anne watched, seething with jealousy as Mary and Daphne pulled themselves protectively near the shivering redhead, taking her hands, rubbing her forehead, whispering into her ears like nurses.

13

I spent a night in the Red Room, and none of them ever even touched me.

"Let it out, Shirley. Go on, you can do it. Let it out."

"I can't . . . it's too horrid. . . ."

"You can, you can!"

"For Christ's sake!" Anne yelled. "Are we doing Lamaze for the dead now? Leave her alone. If it has to, it'll come out. She won't be able to stop it."

Mary turned from her ministrations to look at Anne with that puzzled expression again. "Lamaze?"

"Forget it," Anne said, shaking her head.

In an instant, Shirley pitched out of Daphne and Mary's grasp. She flopped onto her chest and raised her shoulders up by pushing on her hands. Her eyes were fixed on a spot in midair, the way a cat's eyes are when it seems to see what no one else can. All the fear—and for that matter, all other expression—vanished from her face as she began to speak.

A storm raged overhead, pelting the road and the SUV with rain. The family vacation wasn't getting off to the best of starts. It seemed to Lindsay Morgan that the rain was following them, like some kind of nasty omen telling her the family vacation was cursed. The closer to Redlands Beach they got, the louder the rain beat on the car.

With her dad driving and her mom in the passenger seat, Lindsay sat in the back, listening to music on her iPod and texting with her friend Kate. The drive had exhausted her and the storm was doing nothing to improve her mood. She knew the vacation was important to her parents, especially her dad, but Lindsay had spent the last few weeks dreading the trip. It couldn't have come at a worse time. She'd been helping Kate with a totally important party, and now she couldn't even go! Of course, her dad was quick to point out that Lindsay had always enjoyed trips to her uncle Lou's place. But she'd been a little girl then. At sixteen, Lindsay wasn't feeling any glee for the retro.

She was certain her dad just didn't get it. She'd grown up. She was in high school. She was popular and received good grades. Though her teachers sometimes flinched at her often harsh humor, they couldn't help but see the intelligence behind it. Oh, she could be snide and sarcastic, and more than once a friendly burn had been taken as meanness by kids who didn't know her, but it usually only took a few kind words to mend those feelings, and often enough Lindsay found herself with another friend. Plus—and Lindsay felt certain her father did *not* get this—she could take care of herself. When she was faced with a problem, she found a way to fix it. She didn't let it stress her out or piss her off; she just made it work. Lindsay Morgan was practical that way. But she'd tried to fix this trip—had done everything she could to avoid it—and it hadn't worked.

She might not have been so bummed if her parents were taking her to a happening beach like Cancún or the Hamptons or even Atlantic City. But they weren't. They were going to her uncle's house on Redlands Beach, and though it had sand and ocean, it fell way short of an A-list destination. True, Lindsay's memories of the place were a bit fuzzy, but that didn't mean she was wrong. She remembered her uncle and other men standing on the shore with their fishing lines sunk in the ocean (which was probably why his house always smelled like fish guts). There were noisy children racing from the surf toward their chain-smoking mothers and their beer-drinking fathers. The "good" restaurant in town served fried clams in a plastic basket. On reflection, she considered the beach some kind of trailer trash econo-resort, but her folks said it was an up-and-coming town.

She'd asked to stay home, arguing rationally at first. When logical pleas tanked, Lindsay resorted to a more emotional approach. Tears were involved. They didn't work. Anger soon followed, but it didn't get her anywhere. There was no way she could get out of the trip. Her parents had already taken the time off work. So Lindsay was faced with ten days in her uncle's house—away from her friends and an epic party.

Just thinking about it made her sad. Everyone from school was going to be there. BlackBerrys and cell phones had been buzzing about it for weeks. All the cool and cute would be gathering at Kate's house. (*Her* parents were vacationing in Paris!) It would be a red carpet event with beer and banging tunes, and Lindsay was going to miss it.

Lindsay's motivations weren't totally selfish either. Yes, she badly wanted to go—who wouldn't?—but Kate needed her, *really* needed her, and that was important, too.

Lindsay loved her friend like a sister, but Kate was about as organized as a chimp, not to mention the fact that she was panic waiting to happen. Lindsay knew the second one little thing went wrong with the party, Kate would freak like a meth head on *Cops*. She had said a billion times she couldn't pull the party off without Lindsay.

The invitation tragedy was a perfect example. Kate had wanted to use paper invitations, and that would have been okay, but she bought boxes of invites with a picture of a kitten wearing sunglasses on the cover. Inside they read, "Come and party with the cool cats." If Kate had sent out those wholly cred-killing invites, she'd never have lived down the humiliation. So Lindsay wrote the invitation for Kate—email only—and she made it sound like a total secret, because Lindsay knew the best way to get the word out was to tell people to keep quiet.

Lindsay often thought that she would make a great party planner, or maybe a wedding planner. She was able to look at any event, no matter how complicated, calmly and thoroughly, and spot the details others might overlook. Last year she organized the freshman dance, and instead of throwing some high-school hoedown with a pop tune theme, she made it memorable. She did an industrial disco night called Batcave, with painted wall panels that made the gym look like a dungeon and a wrought-iron bar for sodas. It was a total hit. Everyone at school talked about it for weeks.

Kate just can't do this on her own. I should be there, helping her.

But she wasn't; she was in an SUV with her parents, driving through a downpour headed to Redneck Hollow, and no matter how she tried to hide her disappointment—because she knew the trip really meant a lot to her dad—she just couldn't.

It was like being kidnapped or something. She was a prisoner, and her two captors sat in the front seat, acting all happy and crap.

When the power on her Treo died, cutting off Lindsay in midtext, she couldn't help but groan. Her connection to home and her friends was severed. She hadn't bothered charging her cell phone completely, because she preferred the PDA. So her cell phone had died an hour into the trip, and now her Treo was toast. How much worse was this trip going to get?

A hand touched her shoulder, and Lindsay looked up, startled. Her mom had turned in the seat and was looking at her with a shadow of frustration on her brow. Her mom's lips were moving, but Lindsay couldn't hear what she said because she had her tunes cranked. She pulled the earbuds out and said, "What?"

"You know, you could talk to us if you're bored."

"I could, but that would negate the whole not-talking-to-you thing."

Her dad laughed, and her mother just shook her head.

"We're sorry about Kate's party," her dad said. "But try to have a good time. You used to love the beach."

She really wished he'd quit saying that.

"I also used to wear diapers, but I don't see any of us clinging to that tradition."

"You'll feel better when we get there. Believe me, it's nicer now."

Lindsay rested her head against the cold window. The vibrations from the road and the rain beating down massaged her temple. Outside, the day grew darker, and the downpour rapped harder on the SUV's roof. All she could see were blurry trees and more blurry trees, the same view over and over, like an animated message board avatar.

Of course, there was a major difference. She was trapped in this image.

Lindsay sat in the SUV while her parents shopped at the grocery store on the edge of town. She'd tried to see the city's shops and offices through the storm, but everything outside the car was a big gloomy smear. So she searched her iPod for a song—not a specific song, just one that might make her feel better. Scrolling along the titles, she came across a cool tune by Green Day and jabbed the Play button, but after listening to a few grinding guitar riffs, she poked the button again and turned it off.

Lindsay pulled the earbuds loose, wrapped them around her iPod, and dropped the player on the seat. She crossed her arms and leaned back against the door, staring at the front of the supermarket. *Come on, Dad*, she thought, watching the glass doors slide open and closed for shoppers. *Hurry up*.

She felt certain her mood would improve when they reached the house. The SUV and the storm felt so confining. She would have gone into the store with her parents, except her mom would have constantly asked her opinion about food and junk to make Lindsay feel involved, and she just wasn't in the mood. The house would be better. She could charge up her phone and Treo and reconnect with Kate so her friend didn't have an attack over the party. And bonus, her uncle Lou was out of town. That was such a relief. Lou wasn't a total freak, but he came close. He was loud and annoying and told the worst knock-knock jokes ever. Her dad said he was in Arkansas, fishing with friends, which meant she'd get the guest room, and her parents would take his. At least she'd have some privacy.

But what was she supposed to do for ten days? She couldn't hang with her parents the whole time, though she imagined that was her dad's plan.

"You might meet a nice boy on the beach," her mom had said before they left on the trip.

Yeah right, Lindsay thought. *Redlands Beach is probably crawling with gap-toothed Cletuses. Likely they swim in cutoff jeans and show off their hairy backs. Gross.*

She smiled and shook her head, but she did find a ray of hope way in the back of her thoughts. Maybe she *would* meet a boy. It could happen. People from all over went to the beach in the summer.

The glass doors of the store opened. Lindsay squinted through the storm and saw a fat guy in overalls hauling two bags of groceries into the downpour. Sadly, that was the kind of guy who'd probably be prowling the beach, his round belly rolling over the top of his swim trunks. Or worse, what if he was feeling saucy and decided to wear a thong?

Lindsay groaned and laughed, imagining that very thing. "So sick," she whispered to the empty car.

Though totally unlikely, some hot guy's parents might have kidnapped him, too. That would be cool. They'd meet on the beach. He'd have blond hair and aquamarine swimming trunks, like the kind she saw that *OC* stud wearing in last night's rerun. His name would be something totally cool, like Jaimie or Josh, and he'd be eighteen and headed off to college after summer. Every afternoon they'd meet on the beach and then hit town for coffee and stuff.

As she thought this, the doors of the market slid open again. Two men stood in the opening, side by side. One was tall and slender, the other short and round. The rain blurred their faces, so Lindsay only got a vague impression of what they looked like. Both wore slick black parkas against the rain. The round one held a sack of groceries. The thin one opened an umbrella, then handed it to the round man. The thin man opened a second umbrella that he raised over his head, and the two men stepped into the storm.

They walked slowly, seeming to match each

other's steps perfectly in a creepy kind of dance. The mushroom parts of the umbrellas floated over their heads, gliding smoothly through the battering rain and wind. Lindsay squinted harder and slid across the seat to get a better look at these strange men. A chill ran down her back, and her hands trembled.

When the men reached the front of her parents' SUV, the tall one looked through the windshield at her. His head turned slowly, though his shoulders didn't move. He didn't stop walking, didn't even pause. He kept looking at her, though. His narrow face was blank and motionless, his eyes black with shadows. And his head kept turning, as if it wasn't attached to the rest of him.

Lindsay's stomach knotted with fear. The guy was creeping her out bad. She checked the doors and made sure they were locked; then she curled her legs up tight to her chest and held them with her arms. She looked down at the screen of her iPod and stared at the letters without reading them. Anything to distract herself from the curious freaks with umbrellas. She counted to ten, feeling certain that at any moment she'd hear the sound of the door handle click and crack as the two men in black tried to break into the car.

On the number nine, with her heart beating so hard she thought it would burst through her chest, a loud rapping startled her, and she yelped. Her head whipped up, away from the iPod screen, and she saw her dad's face, dripping wet, pressed up against the glass. He was pointing at the door lock and shouting, "Hurry up."

Lindsay sprang forward to disengage the lock. Behind her dad, she saw the two men in black drifting deeper into the storm.

As they drove south on the narrow coastal road, Lindsay was thrilled to see all of the new construction going up near town. Then she was disappointed when they neared her uncle's house, because this stretch hardly seemed to have changed at all. Every tenth house was fantastic— all glass and new paint—which only served to point out the lameness of the older properties.

Of course, the weather didn't help. It was so dreary. Still, she kept hoping, unreasonably that in the years since she'd last visited the beach it had gone from zero to hero on the resort scale. Then, just before turning into her uncle's drive, she saw the sign for the Redlands Mobile Home Park, and her spirits sank a little lower.

Lightning cracked as Lindsay followed her parents into Uncle Lou's house. The rain sounded like a million tiny footsteps on the roof.

"It's supposed to clear up tomorrow," her dad said. He carried her bags upstairs, while her mom stayed in the kitchen to unload the groceries.

Uncle Lou's house hadn't changed in five years. His green sofa still faced the fireplace in the den, and the square wooden coffee table sat in front of it. He still had all of the old paintings of dogs and hunters on the walls. At least he'd discovered the magic of Febreze, so the room didn't smell as bad as she remembered. Lindsay went to the window and looked toward the beach. Angry surf, with caps of froth, cut a line through the otherwise gray scene. The beach looked messy with tons of driftwood and litter poking out of the sand.

Glad I brought sandals. I'd cut my toes to shreds on that stuff.

Once she heard her dad's heavy feet on the stairs, Lindsay turned away from the view. She needed to recharge her Treo, cell phone, and iPod, and get her laptop set up.

Her dad met her at the bottom of the stairs and

said, "You're all set. First door on the right. Why don't you get unpacked and then come down to help your mom fix dinner?"

"I have to call Kate first," Lindsay said, walking up the stairs. "Tell Mom I'll do the salad."

The room wasn't awful. The bed was huge, with a fluffy down quilt hugging the top of the mattress. A small chest of drawers, hardly large enough for the clothes she brought, stood by the closet. There was a cool window seat with a thick green cushion on the far side of the bed. She imagined that was where she'd spend a lot of the next ten days, drinking coffee and looking out at the ocean or at the screen of her laptop. That would work. She could picture herself there, like one of those models in a coffee commercial, looking all cool and content while gripping a steaming mug of bean and gazing out into the world.

There was even an electrical outlet built into the wall under the window seat, so she could keep her laptop plugged in. Nice.

Lindsay lifted the first suitcase onto the bed, where it sank in the fluffy quilt. She unpacked her cables and chargers first, plugging them into the socket by the chest of drawers, and then connected her cell phone and iPod. She carried her laptop and its power cord to the window seat and hooked them up.

Looking out the window, she noticed the house next door. It was smaller than her uncle's house, and it looked like it might just collapse under the next big gust of wind. The shingles were black and torn like the scales of a sick dragon. The house was supposed to be white, but the boards were dirty and broken. The porch in front sagged, and the two windows on the side facing her were crusted with dirt. The gloomy afternoon made it hard to tell exactly how dismal the house was, but viewed through the rain, the place made her uncle's house look like a Malibu palace.

Movement caught her eye, and Lindsay looked into the backyard. The first thing she noticed was the umbrella—a large black mushroom, opened up to keep its owner dry. She could not see who stood beneath the umbrella, but he wore a slick black parka just like the ones the men from the grocery store wore. The umbrella guy stood beneath a scraggly tree with pointy limbs. He didn't move, just faced the back of the house like a black statue.

Uneasy again, Lindsay stepped away from the window seat. What if the freaky umbrella guys had followed her? What if they lived *next door*? The place had all the charm of a zombie hostel, so it wouldn't be hard to believe.

She finished unpacking her things and returned to the window seat. Cautiously, she looked at the house next door. The umbrella guy was gone, and she found that even creepier than seeing him standing under the skeletal tree. He could be any-where. He could be looking at her right now.

Lindsay backed away from the window. At the chest of drawers she lifted her cell phone, which was still connected to the charging cord, and dialed Kate's number with a trembling finger.

"Get me out of here," she said when Kate picked up.

"That bad, huh?"

"Worse."

Kate giggled. In the background, the TV blared some sitcom, and her friend's laughter blended with the show's laugh track.

"There's this house next door," Lindsay said, "and Buffy wouldn't go into it. And there are these weird guys with umbrellas all over town."

"Is it raining?"

"Yeah, it's raining, but these are huge black umbrellas and all of the guys have these shiny black parkas on. It's like they're part of a cult or something."

"Maybe they don't want to get wet."

"You'd understand if you saw them. They're from some serial killer outlet store. One of them was just outside, and he was totally scoping me."

That was a lie, but she had to say something so Kate would understand just how bizarre these guys were.

"No way," Kate said.

"So true. He was in back of the place next door, just staring. Totally not moving or anything. Just staring."

"Is he still there?"

"No. He bailed."

"Weird."

"I know. It's just awful here."

"It sounds like it," Kate said. "Maybe it'll be better if you get some sun."

"I hope so. Right now it's just so gray."

"Have you forgiven your parents yet?"

"Not even. They must be punished. I canNOT

believe they picked this week to drag me out of town."

"Well, you totally helped with the party. I so owe you, big."

"It's okay. I just wish I could be there. It's going to be way fun."

"I'm so nervous."

"You'll do fine. Just make sure you have the number of the taxi company if anyone gets too wasted, and do not let Justin and Farge in."

"Oh my god," Kate said with a cackling laugh. "I'd have to fumigate the place if those burners got in."

"Exactly," Lindsay said. "Just remember, they are guests in your house, but it is *your* house. Don't put up with any dis'."

"I won't, Linds. Thanks so much. I totally have to go like now. I'll call you tomorrow, okay?"

"See ya."

Back at the window, Lindsay sat on the edge of the green cushion and looked out. The yard next door was still empty. She relaxed a bit and opened up her laptop. Kate was probably right. It *was* raining really hard, and it made sense that people would have umbrellas and raincoats on. It wasn't like a total breakdown in reality.

As she thought this, a figure dashed into the alley, pushing close to the rundown house. Lindsay pulled a little way back, just looking over the edge of the sill to see who stood below.

The boy was blond with long frayed dreadlocks. He wore cargo shorts, Teva sandals, and a tie-dyed T-shirt that was drenched and pasted to his body. He bent at the waist, and a flash of light burst over his belly as he sparked a lighter. Hunched over, the burner was sparking a bowl in the downpour.

What a looz, Lindsay thought. The burner couldn't even wait to get home and get under some shelter before taking a hit.

The boy straightened up a bit, cupping his pipe in his palm so it didn't get too wet. He exhaled a thick cloud of smoke that was immediately beat down by the rain. Lifting his face to let the downpour wash over him, looking ecstatic, the boy shoved the pipe into a pocket. Lindsay moved farther from the window. She so didn't want this dope jockey spotting her.

He started walking to the back of the house, pausing at a window and looking in.

Lindsay'd had enough. She turned away from the window and focused her attention on her laptop. She checked her email, but there was nothing interesting: a piece of spam from one of those online pharmacy places, a notice from Amazon that her DVD order was shipping, and a note from her friend Trey.

Like Kate, Trey had been Lindsay's friend forever. He was just so nice. She'd never heard him say a nasty thing about anyone. It was like he liked everyone, and he always said the sweetest things. Lindsay knew he'd kind of crushed on her for a while in the eighth grade, but then he'd met Sarah Thomas during the summer break, and by the time he'd come back for the ninth grade he was in love with Sarah. Unfortunately, the relationship ended last year, when Sarah moved to California with her family. Trey had been miserable, and Lindsay had felt miserable for him. But she'd taken him out for coffee every day for two weeks, letting him unload his sadness on her, and soon enough his smile was back.

She looked at his email and smiled. For the tenth time in three days, he told her how much he would miss her at Kate's party. She'd run out of ways to thank him, so she simply replied with a smiley emoticon.

She reminded herself that she needed to run downstairs and help her mom with dinner, but for the moment she just wanted some quiet. Lindsay scooted back on the window seat and leaned against the wall. Just then a light came on in the house next door. She leaned closer to the window, close enough that her breath made fog on the glass. The burner was gone, probably dancing over the sand, too high to care about the storm. The light came from the second window about halfway back on the house. Someone moved in the room, throwing shadows up and down the wall. Lindsay wiped a cloud of vapor from the glass.

Then she saw him. The distance and rain made it impossible for Lindsay to make out any details, but a boy came to the window, and she saw *him*. So not the pot-smoking looz. Black hair. A slender muscular build. He was wearing distressed jeans and no shirt, and even through the gloom, she could see his developed pecs and six-pack abs. She pushed as close to the glass as she could to see if his face was as fine as she wanted it to be, but the weather smoothed the specifics of his features, leaving nothing but an impression of the boy, a very hot impression.

Suddenly the family vacation was looking a lot better.

At dinner Lindsay was in better spirits. She ate and joked with her mom and dad. As parents went, Lindsay knew she had it good. Her mom and dad were still married, still in love. They still had sex way too much, and she *soooo* didn't want to think about that. But at least they hadn't split like so many of her friends' parents had, and despite having dragged her on this vacation, they usually let her do her own thing and didn't gripe too much. They rarely yelled at her and didn't pull cheap stunts like snagging her cell phone as punishment (an art Kate's mother had perfected).

"Your mom wants to go flea marketing tomorrow," her dad said, before raising a fork full of corn to his mouth. He chewed and drank some wine. Then he said, "You feel like coming along, or do you want to check out the beach?"

Winnie the Pooh, Lindsay thought. Her dad looked like Winnie the Pooh. He had a round face, and when he smiled his cheeks pooched out. His eyebrows were really thin and neat, but the rest of his face was rounded and blunt. Pooh had been her favorite cartoon character when she was a little girl. Strange that she'd never noticed the resemblance before.

He had his eyebrows arched and grinned like he was waiting for the punch line of a joke. Lindsay almost laughed at the expression.

"I'm going to hang here," she said. Her dad's smile faded into disappointment. "I'm going to be on panic alert with Kate until her party is over. She's kind of counting on the long distance help. I'll just hang and explore the beach or something. You guys have fun."

"We won't be out long," her mom said.

"Cool," Lindsay said. "If the weather is still crappy, I can watch the box."

"It's supposed to be clear and warm," her dad said. "I'll bet the beach will be swarming with kids."

"Well, they better stay on the beach," her mom said. "I don't want you bringing strangers into your uncle's house unless we're here to meet them."

Lindsay rolled her eyes and put her fork down. "Right, because I want a bunch of slack-jawed mouth breathers to know where I'm staying." She smiled widely to show her parents she was just playing.

"You might be surprised," her dad said. "I told you the real estate market has been booming in this area. A lot of new people have moved in, and a lot of tourists are renting houses for the summer. Your uncle told me it's quite the resort town these days."

Sure, Lindsay thought. *It's Cancún and Ibiza all rolled into one. That's why there's a trailer park half a mile up the beach.*

Still, she realized it was better than she'd thought. There had been new shops downtown, and some of the houses were new and cool. And of course the bit of eye candy next door didn't hurt.

Though she'd only caught a glimpse of him, she thought about the boy, wondered if he were visiting or if his parents owned the house. She reminded herself that she hadn't seen him very well. Close-up he might look like Freddy Krueger, or he might be old, like twenty-five or something. But she didn't think so. He might be a couple years older than her, and maybe he wasn't a total CW throbber, but he could be.

"Did Uncle Lou say who owned the house next door?" Lindsay asked, making sure she sounded really casual.

"No," her dad said. "I know he was pretty upset when Don and Judy sold the place, but that was over a year ago. He hasn't said a word about the new owners."

"And what's so interesting about the house next door?" her mom asked.

Lindsay knew she couldn't say anything about the boy without enduring her mom's goofy jokes about romance, so she didn't. "Someone needs to introduce them to *Total House Makeover*," she said.

"It could use a bit of renovation," her dad agreed. "I noticed the porch was missing a couple of boards when we were unloading the car. It's a shame. The structure looks pretty solid. The place could be real nice with a little work."

"Maybe a bulldozer would help," Lindsay joked.

"Be nice. It's not that bad," her mom said.

"I have exacting standards and exquisite taste. As such I can't help but notice how much most things blow."

Her dad laughed loudly, and her mom smiled.

"That's my girl," her dad announced, and jabbed his fork into a piece of chicken.

She found the binoculars on the windowsill in the den. Lindsay certainly wasn't looking for them, but there they were. After dinner she'd wandered into the room, wanting to see more of the ocean. She picked the glasses up and lifted them to her eyes. The metal casing was heavy and cold against her soft skin. Looking through the lenses, she adjusted the focus until the distant ocean waves came to her crisp and clear, though still terribly gray from the storm. Breakers rose and crashed and foamed. It looked cool, if depressing. She swept the glasses over the horizon and down the beach, where she again adjusted the focus, bringing a new object into view.

"Jeez," Lindsay yelped, tearing the glasses from her eyes. There was something hideous and unbelievable out there. It looked like a baby, buried in the sand.

She looked through the binoculars again and relaxed. It was a doll. The plastic head was crushed and most of the body was buried in wet sand, but its sad and mangled face was clear enough. One of the eyes was open, while the other was covered with the broken eyelid, which drooped askance against the doll's cheek. The plastic fibers that once looked like hair fanned over the sand, dirty and wet.

Farther along, she saw the side of a distant house and then a window. Lindsay adjusted the focus yet again, and nearly dropped the binoculars when the image cleared.

A woman, maybe her mom's age but totally beautiful, walked through the upstairs bedroom of the house. She wore a brightly colored piece of fabric knotted around her waist. Its lovely purple and crimson swirls draped to the woman's knees. Besides the loose skirt, the woman was naked.

Embarrassed, Lindsay put the binoculars back on the sill and stepped away. It occurred to her that the half-naked woman was the exact reason her uncle Lou kept the binoculars on the sill, and she shuddered at the idea.

Still, she might be able to use the binoculars.

She wouldn't watch the boy next door, wouldn't spy on him or anything. But at least she could get a good look at him. More than likely he'd turn out to be just another guy, and that would be that. Though if he was cute . . .

The thing was, Lindsay had to take something good back from this trip, even if it was just a story about the hot guy next door. Her parents had dragged her away from the party of the year. That's all anyone would talk about when she got home, and Lindsay would feel like a complete shadow if she didn't have an equally cool—no, cooler—story to tell. She needed an adventure or a summer romance, something none of the other kids would have. She couldn't go home with stories about flea markets or rubbing suntan lotion on her mom's back.

Lindsay left the binoculars on the windowsill and walked through the dining room to the kitchen door. Wanting to make sure her parents were busy before she lifted the binoculars, Lindsay pushed open the swinging door and froze.

Her stomach knotted up, and she reared back a step. Her parents were making out against the kitchen counter.

They weren't just kissing either. That was gross enough, but they were really lip-locked, and her mom had her hand inside her dad's shirt, rubbing his stomach. She didn't even want to think about where her dad's hands were.

At least they'd be busy for a while.

Lindsay closed the door quietly. She grabbed the binoculars and went up to her room.

Lindsay stood next to the window seat, adjusting the binoculars, focusing on the window of the house next door, but she didn't see the boy. The light was out in his room and not so much as a shadow moved. After a few minutes, she felt like a perv, and hid the binoculars under the green cushion before logging onto the web. She surfed around for a while, but the long day had exhausted her, and soon enough she turned off her computer and crossed the hall to the bathroom to brush her teeth.

Ten minutes later, she lay in bed and stared at the ceiling. The house was so quiet she could hear music playing next door. It was strange. It sounded New Agey, with the muffled chime of bells and a small drum being rapped beneath a moaning melody like chanting. Maybe the kid's grandparents were hippies or something. Her friend Trey's grandparents were like that. They wore headbands and said things like "groovy," "peace," and "far out" a lot. They really liked a place called Woodstock and a band called Happy Dead or something like that. Of course, Lindsay had no idea what that band sounded like. They might be just like the odd monotone voices she was hearing, punctuated by chimes and drums. They probably were.

Don't let it be his music, she thought. How sad would that be? A hot guy who listened to decaf tunes? That would be tear-worthy.

The moaning chant rose in volume, sounding deep and ominous.

Then a cry pierced through the muffled music. It sounded like someone was in pain. And it didn't seem to be part of the drum and chant song. Lindsay looked at the window, worried. Did someone outside need help?

Is it part of the song?

Afraid, Lindsay curled up tightly under the covers. The sound didn't come again, though she strained to hear. After a while, the music stopped and the night grew silent. Then she rolled over, faced the wall, and waited for sleep to come.

Lindsay woke to sunshine, the fear of the night forgotten. A wedge of golden light fell through the window, cutting a swath across the room and the end of her bed. Her parents moved around in their room at the other end of the hall. She heard their footsteps and their voices. Her mom giggled, and her dad made a growling noise. Lindsay did her best to ignore them. She felt great. Rested. Clearheaded. She wanted to pretend she was alone in this house and shared the beach with no one but the boy next door.

Lindsay rolled over and snuggled deeper into the quilt. He would be hot, she decided. No way did he listen to that hippie music. He would be young and cool and totally into extreme sports. A guy didn't get a body like that by playing video games all day. He was probably at the beach to surf. So cool. And he wouldn't be one of the immature guys she met at school. He'd be an adult, but not too old. *He'll be perfect,* she thought. *Just perfect.*

When she finally left her fantasy behind and got out of bed, she powered up her laptop and cast a glance out the window. No one moved in the yard or behind the windows of the rundown house. Disappointed, she grabbed her robe and put it on. Downstairs she found her parents in the kitchen again, only this time they weren't macking all over each other. That was a relief.

They exchanged good mornings and her dad, still smiling, asked if she'd slept well.

"Pretty good," she replied, heading directly for the coffeepot.

"It's the sea air."

"Mmmm," Lindsay replied, already deeply involved with her first cup of bean.

"I'm fixing pancakes," her mom said.

"Mom," Lindsay said, "you know I don't eat breakfast."

"You're on vacation."

"Try to convince my thighs," Lindsay said. "Thanks anyway. Coffee is fine."

She took her coffee upstairs and carried it to the window seat. After getting situated with her computer in her lap and her coffee next to her hip, she opened her email, but the house next door kept distracting her. She read a line of one of Trey's messages, looked down at the window, read another line. Kate sent an email telling her that Nick Faherty—only the hottest guy at school— was definitely going to be at her party and . . . *OMG, do you believe it? He's bringing his older brother who looks just like Tom Welling. I wish you could come. I'm going to be a total head case.*

Yes, you will, Lindsay thought. She looked through the window, thought she saw movement across the way, but the boy didn't appear.

Lindsay clicked the Reply button so she could tell Kate how happy she was for her. Nick and Ian Faherty were quite a party coup. It was epically unfair that Lindsay wouldn't be there to hang with them.

Before writing the note, she again looked out

the window and was startled to see two men looking up at her from the backyard of the unpleasant
house. The sight of them was unnerving. They just
stood there, staring. But what really got to her was
the fact that they were the same guys she'd seen
at the grocery store wearing black parkas and
holding huge umbrellas.

Today they wore black T-shirts and gray shorts.
Both men seemed to be several years older than
her dad but in infinitely better shape. The day
before, she thought they were exact opposites,
one skinny and one fat, but now she could see
their muscle through their tight shirts. The short
one was so buffed it looked like his shirt would
tear open if he moved his arms at all. The tall one
was narrower but ripped.

Lindsay looked away, hoping she hadn't stared
too long. It was freaky enough to have them looking at her; she certainly didn't want to get caught
staring back.

A thought began to emerge as she gazed at the
blank email template on her screen. Maybe the
boy next door had two fathers. He was the son of
a gay couple. How cool would that be? Her friend
Rachel had two moms, and they were really nice.

Maybe the boy was adopted. That made him even more exotic. Another thought tried to creep in—a thought about the boy being something other than a son to these two men—but she pushed that away quickly. Life just couldn't be that unfair.

She threw another quick glance outside. The shorter man was pointing at the base of the house and talking to the taller man, who stooped to hear. The tall guy nodded his head. In the window, thirty feet from where these men examined the run-down house, the boy appeared.

Lindsay's heart raced, and she looked away to her computer screen. *Let him see you first*, she thought. *Don't let him catch you staring. He'll think you're a major freak. Just be cool. Pretend he isn't there and write back to Kate. Flip your hair just a bit, but don't look out the window. Smile like you've just thought of something brilliant. Drink some coffee. Hold the mug at your chin for a moment. Look up like your brilliant thought is totally deep. Put the mug down. Casually look out the window, and . . .*

The boy was gone. The two men in black T-shirts stared up at her from the backyard. Both looked pissed off.

Feeling uncomfortable under their gaze, Lindsay lifted her laptop and carried it with her to the bed so she could write back to Kate.

Lindsay waited for her parents to leave for the flea markets before taking her shower and cleaning up for the day. She stood in front of the chest of drawers looking at the tops and the shorts she'd packed and didn't like any of them. All the clothes looked like something a little girl would wear, all pinks and yellows and whites. This always happened to her. Every time she *needed* to look good, she just couldn't find anything to wear. Most of her clothes were brand-new, but somewhere between the store rack and her uncle's house they'd lost their appeal. None of her outfits looked special enough. What if she ran into the boy outside? She didn't want to look like some Hicksville teen. Crap. These things were all she had, though. Something from the drawer would have to do. Finally she chose a pair of yellow shorts and took a white blouse from the closet.

Once dressed, she returned to the window for a moment to look down, but the boy wasn't there. She wandered downstairs and onto the porch of her uncle's house. The sky was clear and blue and the day hot, though the breeze off the ocean cooled her skin. Not far up the beach, she noticed the crowds. Dozens of people lay under the baking sun, walked over the sand, soaked in the ocean. She looked south and saw a handful of people there as well.

A car engine sputtered into life, and Lindsay backed toward the door. The noise came from behind the house next door, and she imagined the two old guys were going out for a drive. She walked into the house through the den and dining room to the kitchen door. She opened it, but did not step outside. Instead, she leaned on the jamb, making sure she was hidden from the driver's view.

She heard the car back out of the drive. Once she was certain it was far enough down the road, she poked her head out and saw the back of a long silver sedan. Sunlight glinted off its trunk as it rolled to the north. Satisfied that she could not be spotted, Lindsay walked onto the porch all the way to the rail.

On a whim, she walked to the side and looked over the rail down the length of the house to the window where she first saw the boy. From this angle, she couldn't see anything.

Lindsay walked back inside and up the stairs. In her room, she went immediately to the window seat and pressed her face against the glass, looking down at the boy's room.

And there he was.

He stood in the window. His head was lowered, looking at the band of sand separating his house from her uncle's. Lindsay pulled the binoculars from under the green cushion and quickly put them to her eyes. It took way too long for her to adjust the lenses, but finally the boy came into focus.

Excited, she waited for him to look up from the sandy ground. When he did, her throat closed up tight and her heart raced.

He *was* hot. As she expected, he was only a little older than her. Seventeen, maybe eighteen. His black hair jutted in wild spikes from his head. His thin face, flawless and beautiful, wore a sad expression that made Lindsay's heart flutter. His eyes were as blue as the sky. His frowning lips were full, and she suddenly wanted to kiss him, which was totally weird because she didn't even know him.

But she found herself thrilled by the wonderment of what his lips might taste like and feel like against her own.

Lindsay spun from the window, clutching the binoculars to her chest. What was she going to do now? It wasn't like she could just go over to his house and say, "Hey, my parents dragged me out here from the city, and I got bored and was looking through my uncle's binoculars and thought you were hot, so why don't we date or something?"

She could sit in the window seat for a while and pretend to write on her laptop. He might see her, but then, he might not.

Her cell phone rang, yanking Lindsay from her thoughts. She checked the caller ID.

Kate.

"Perfect timing," Lindsay said as she answered the phone.

"What? What's going on?"

"Nine-one-one."

"More scary umbrella men?"

"Noooo," Lindsay said. "Jeez, live in the now. It's male-related."

"Beach hottie?"

"Way hottie. I mean, he's staying in the house next door. I saw him through the window last night, and I thought he might be cute, but then I saw him again today, and he totally is. He's at his window right now."

"Is said hottie age-appropriate?" Kate asked.

"Duh."

"Any sign of female interference?"

"What? Like a girlfriend? I don't think so. The only other people I've seen at the house are a couple of old guys. I think they might be his parents."

"Both of them? Like Rachel's moms?"

"Pre-xactly like that. They're both buff, full-on groomed, and wear matching outfits."

"Sounds totally same-sex to me."

"I know," Lindsay said. "Progressive, right?"

"Do they really wear identical outfits? I mean, is it like they order from the same J.Crew catalogue or is it matching leather diapers or what?"

"Kate, come on."

"Okay," Kate said. "Is he still at the window?"

Lindsay leaned forward just enough to see the boy in the neighboring house. "Yes."

"Well, what are you going to do?"

She thought about it for a moment and came

up with a plan. It was simple and cool. It made her smile. "We're going for a walk," Lindsay said.

"I can't," Lindsay said, standing on the sand behind her uncle's house.

"Well, I know I couldn't, but you can," Kate said. "You can do anything. Besides, it's no crisis. You're just talking on the phone, wandering around the yard. No big deal. You don't even know he exists. It's a total coincidence. Now, set to steppin'. I have a bazillion things to do before the party."

"I'm so pissed I can't be there."

"I know," Kate said. "It's totally lame. There's no way I can pull this off without you here. I mean, what if we run out of beer or something? Or what if Matt starts a fight? Crap. I should just cancel."

"You can't cancel. If you're worried about the beer, just have Matt's brother pick up a couple of extra cases. Put them in the bathroom off the kitchen, in the tub, and cover them with ice. As for Matt, he isn't going to start a fight, because his mother threatened to yank him off the basketball team if he caused any more trouble. If he gets all weird, just remind him of that."

"I will," Kate said. "You're right. Thanks."

"No problem."

"I promise I'll take a ton of pictures and post them on my website. It'll be kind of like being there."

"Uh-huh." And watching the Oscars on television was kind of like being Colin Farrell's date. "Now, I'm about to make contact."

Lindsay shook out her free hand to relieve a bit of stress. She rolled her head on her neck and then stepped onto the band of sand between the two houses. Though she tried to resist, she threw a quick glance at the boy's window. Catching herself, she looked away quickly before she could even tell if he was there. Instead she looked down and noticed for the first time that her uncle's house didn't rest on the ground. It stood three feet above the sand on wooden supports. In the shadows under the house, tufts of tall grasses grew.

"That's weird," she said.

"What? Is he gross close-up?"

"No," Lindsay said. "We've come to my uncle's a bunch of times before, and I never noticed that his house is built up off the ground."

"Yeah, fascinating," Kate said, her voice thick with sarcasm. "Architecture is hot. What's *the boy* doing?"

"I haven't looked over there yet. Should I?"

"Yeah, but let me say something funny first. That way, he'll see you smiling."

"Okay."

"On the count of three," Kate said. "Ready? One, two . . ."

Lindsay began to turn, hoping the boy would still be in his window when she completed the turn.

"Three," Kate said. "Michael Chandler."

Lindsay broke into a wide smile at the mention of the name. Last year, Brett Underhill had dragged Kate into the boy's locker room as a prank, and she'd seen more than a couple of the boys undressed, including Michael Chandler. Chandler was a big mean jock who liked to beat up the younger kids, and Kate got a full monty look at him. In her words, his unit was like a pencil eraser in a nest of black thread. But Michael Chandler wasn't the point. The point was, Lindsay completed her turn with a huge grin on her face.

And the boy was in his window, looking out at her. She froze, absolutely froze solid when she saw him.

"Did it work?" Kate asked. "Lindsay? Hey? Is he there?"

"Um . . . uhm-hmm."

He was definitely there. The boy smiled back and lifted a hand in greeting.

Lindsay tried to return the wave, but her arm felt like it weighed a hundred pounds. He was just so good-looking. He looked like a movie star, only better because he was real and present and separated from her by nothing but a piece of dirty glass. Through the binoculars, she thought his eyes were the color of sky, but they were lighter than that, so light. So amazing.

"Lindsay? What is going on?"

"I'll call you back."

"What? Hold on—"

Lindsay killed the signal and put the phone in the pocket of her jeans. The boy next door lifted a finger in the air: one second. He disappeared for a minute, bending down like he was putting something away, then reappeared. He stood up. He was so tall. Lindsay noticed that like the men she saw in the yard that morning, he too wore a black T-shirt, but his was way too big on him. It hung like a tent from his shoulders. He was way too tight-bodied for such a mammoth shirt. Nervous, she looked up and down the band of sand, to the back of the houses and then to the front and the beach and ocean beyond. People were gathered on the sand in front of her uncle's house. Towels and chairs sat beneath a dozen different people, but none of them mattered. Not now.

She looked back at him.

He was waving for her to come closer.

Todd Lombard was Lindsay's first real boyfriend. He was a slender boy with short blond hair, green eyes, and too much brain for his own good. He was Einstein smart and would have been considered a total geek if he hadn't been the star of her middle school's soccer team. Todd was cute and fun, but he was also a little crazy, and not in the fun, let's-raise-some-hell kind of way. Todd heard voices. They told him to do things. They told him jokes, causing Todd to burst out laughing in the middle of algebra or social sciences. Fortunately Lindsay broke it off six months before his parents sent him away to a school in the next county that was able to handle "special" kids like Todd.

Her second boyfriend was normal enough. Too normal. David Carter was also blond and also a soccer player, but he was as dull as a Josh Groban record. All he ever wanted to do was sit around playing video games. When they did go out, they went to movies, usually the ones inspired by video games.

And those two made up Lindsay's romantic history. Neither were bad guys, but they weren't exactly the stuff of great romances either. Still, she had felt an electric charge when they first asked her out. It started in her chest and spread out, shooting up to her scalp and down to her toes. She felt that kind of charge now, walking toward the boy's window, but the voltage was cranked way up, and she didn't know how she could stand this kind of feeling if it went on much longer.

The boy was still smiling at her. His eyes twinkled like he wanted to tell her a secret, but he did not move forward to open the window. She thought that was odd. He stood back from the wall, waving her closer but made no move to slide back the glass that separated them.

Maybe he's sick, she thought. *He could be contagious. He might even be dying. God, wouldn't that suck? It would be kind of romantic, but in a completely awful way.*

When she reached the closed window, she didn't know what to do. She looked up at him, laughed a nervous laugh, and shrugged.

"Hello," he called through the glass.

"Hey," she said.

"What's your name?" the boy asked.

"Lindsay."

"Great name."

"Thanks. What's yours?"

"Mark," he said.

"Hey, Mark."

"Hey."

She felt really stupid talking through the closed window and wondered why he didn't open it.

As if reading her mind, he said, "Stupid window."

"Is it broken?" she asked.

"No," Mark said. "It's hard to explain. You can open it if you want."

Lindsay shrugged and reached out to grasp a thin strip of metal on the outer frame of the glass. As she pulled the window open, she noticed an odd metal bracket fixed in the corner of the window frame. It was made of iron and had a strange shape, swirls and lines in a circle with three points poking away from the center. They weren't very pretty, but at least they were small, hardly bigger than a nickel. One point aimed up the wall, while the other was pointed across the sill. The third jutted toward the center of the window. She noticed another bracket affixed to the inside corner of the sill. In fact, all of the corners, inside and out, wore similar ornaments.

Lindsay stepped away from the open window. She looked inside and saw a small bed pushed against the far wall. A simple blanket lay over the top of it. To her left, on the same wall as the window, was a black upright piano with a narrow bench. *(He's a musician!)* The walls were bare, but there was a desk in front of the window and a pile of clothes against the closet door.

Where is his PC?

"Thank you," Mark said. "This is the first fresh air I've had in days."

"Are you grounded or something?"

"Yeah. Something like that."

"That blows."

"Does it?" he asked. His face scrunched up like

64

he was confused; then he smiled again and nodded his head. "Okay. I understand. Yeah. It definitely blows."

"What did you do?"

"Things," Mark said. "Little stuff mostly. A few plagues and a war or two. Nothing apocalyptic."

Lindsay laughed. "So your parents totally overreact, too?"

"Oh yeah."

"I saw a couple of guys outside this morning. Are they your dads?"

"They are . . ." Mark searched for the right word and decided on, "complicated. They're my guardians, if that's what you mean."

"I guess. They look pretty harsh."

"You don't know the half of it. Doug—he's the tall one—and Jack are seriously cold." He chuckled a dry, humorless laugh and dropped his head. "So, how long have you lived next door? I haven't noticed you before."

"Well, maybe you haven't been paying attention."

"I think you'd get my attention pretty quick."

Lindsay felt herself blush. She looked away from Mark, toward the beach where even more people had gathered in the few minutes since she last looked. When she returned her gaze to Mark, her heart was beating so fast she thought she might faint.

"You didn't answer my question," he said.

"We're just visiting. It's my uncle's house. We got in yesterday."

"Oh, okay. I've seen your uncle around, I think. Skinny guy? Always wearing a trucker cap?"

"That's Uncle Lou."

"How long are you staying?"

"Ten days."

"That's not very long," Mark said. "I was kind of hoping you'd be here for the summer. Who knows, I might actually get out of here one of these days."

"I wish we were staying longer, too," Lindsay said.

Yesterday it would have been a lie, but right now she meant it.

"It gets a little lonely around here. I mean, Doug and Jack are less than entertaining."

"I heard music last night," Lindsay said, choosing her words carefully. "I haven't heard anything like it before."

"Oh man," Mark said with a laugh. "Isn't that the

most awful crap you've ever heard?"

"Yes," Lindsay agreed, thrilled to know it wasn't Mark's music. "It's like a song for a bad yoga studio commercial."

"Totally," Mark said, really laughing now.

"Ugh," Lindsay said.

She searched for something else to say about it, but her mind was blank. Mark kept looking at her with that amazing smile, and she could tell he wanted her to keep talking, but she didn't have a clue what to say. Looking away from him, hoping that her mind would clear without the distraction of his face, Lindsay looked down at the sand, following its ridges and grooves with her eyes.

Say something, she thought, only she didn't know if she meant it for herself or Mark. It didn't really matter. She simply wanted the uncomfortable silence to pass. When Mark remained silent, she forced herself to say, "So, if you weren't grounded, what kinds of stuff would you be doing?"

"Today?" Mark said. "I'd probably be surfing. It's not a great day for it—only two- to four-foot swells. I mean, a couple days back when the storm was coming in, they were slammin', but it's kind of quiet. Still, it's waves and board. A hell of a lot better than walls and bed."

"Cool," Lindsay said. "I'd love to learn how to surf."

"It's great," Mark said. "Other than that, I just kind of hang these days. I used to ski and play football and stuff, but that's kind of over. Doug and Jack aren't what you'd call athletic types."

"They look pretty athletic."

Mark made a *phfft* noise with his lips. "They lift weights and jog, but they aren't into human sports, you know? They aren't out in the world, sharing the slopes and the streets. I mean, there's a world full of people, and if you aren't among them, affecting them, enjoying them, you might as well not exist. It's a total nonlife, and they embrace it because they're afraid."

"Afraid of what?" Lindsay asked.

"I don't know. Just life," Mark said. "Doug and Jack want everything to be controlled and perfect, and the only way to get that is to stay away from real people and real life. They don't understand that chaos and control are the fuel mix that keeps the world spinning. It's screwed up. They're totally removed. Unfortunately, they decided to remove me, too."

"And there's no place else you could go?" she asked.

"Not now," Mark said. His face grew serious, darkened. "Right now, I'm trapped."

"I'm sorry."

"Thanks. It's a temporary situation, but it feels like it's been going on forever." Mark's face brightened. "But now I've met you. You can visit and keep me company every now and then. I mean, when *they* aren't home. They'd totally freak if they knew we were talking."

"Well, then we won't tell them, but maybe I'll stop by again."

Mark's mouth spread into a wide, charming grin. The sight of it just erased Lindsay's cool, and she felt like an excited child. Again she found herself in the middle of a long silence, her mind filled with too many thoughts to pick just one.

"So where do you go to school?" Mark asked.

"Baker High," Lindsay said, then realized Mark would have no idea where that was. "It's in Helensburgh, Pennsylvania."

"I was in PA a couple of times. Philly mostly. It was okay."

"Philadelphia is about an hour away."

"What's Helensburgh like?"

"Kind of like Smallville, only without the hotties."

Mark laughed. "I've been in plenty of those places."

Another uncomfortable silence fell over them.

Lindsay was about to ask how long he and his guardians had lived in the house when she heard their car turning into the drive. Mark's face went from cool and smiling to absolute panic in under a second.

"They're home," Lindsay said, suddenly feeling desperate herself.

"Close the window," Mark said, his voice sharp with fear. "You have to close the window."

"I . . ." Lindsay wanted to run. The car was already parked on the other side of the house. Any second the doors would open, and Mark's guardians might hear them.

"Please," Mark said, drawing away from the desk to the center of the room. "You have to close it."

Lindsay shot her hands out and pushed against the glass until the window was again secure in its frame. She looked at Mark a final time. He mouthed the words *Thank you*.

Then she ran.

5

Lindsay felt so many things. Excitement. Happiness. Disappointment. She paced her living room. Nervous energy crackled in her legs and her fingertips. She needed to keep moving or the energy would burn her up from the inside. But it was all too amazing for her to believe. It was like a fairy tale, only in reverse, because the prince was the one in the tower held captive by his evil guardians. And Mark was as close to a prince as she was likely to find on Redlands Beach. He was handsome and athletic, and he was a musician. Or at least, she assumed he was. He had a piano in his room and little else. It must have been important to him. She should have asked if he played, but she had been so flustered.

She still felt that edgy excitement. She'd wanted an amazing story to tell Kate and everyone when she got home, and now she was living one. Too bad the story had such a sad beginning, with Mark snared by his guardians and all.

He looked so scared, Lindsay thought. *Do they abuse him? Did they hit him? That cry I heard over the music—could that have been Mark? That's totally illegal. Nothing he did could be that bad. Maybe he shoplifted or got caught with a blunt or some beer. He might have borrowed his guardians' car without asking. Kids do stuff like that all the time, but parents act like everything's a murder charge.*

Lindsay stopped pacing for a moment. She looked out the front window at the beach. The water twinkled with silver light as gentle foam-capped waves whispered to the shore. The sun was high above, and the sand was covered with people. She tried to concentrate on the beach-goers in order to undo the knots her emotions had tied in her head and chest.

It didn't work.

♥ ♥ ♥

Lindsay walked on the boardwalk. After meeting Mark, she thought about lying out on the beach, but she was too agitated to just lie down on a towel.

Hot sun bathed her face and shoulders with wonderful warmth. Her sandals clacked on the wooden boards. The boardwalk shops were different than she remembered. Oh, there was still the usual selection of beachwear and surf shops, the flat-front food shacks and the touristy souvenir shops, but now a nice café had sprung up, as well as a clothing store that carried actual fashions, not just T-shirts and bikinis. Not to mention, the buildings were freshly painted. It all looked so much nicer than she remembered it. People wandered in and out of the stores, laughing and pointing, holding hands. Children were everywhere, some clinging close to their parents, others racing back and forth over the boards.

One figure caught her attention—the burner she'd seen outside of her uncle's place yesterday. He stood by the wooden railing across the walk from her. His head was down. Blond dreadlocks formed a thick ragged bush on his scalp.

Lindsay stopped walking. The boy was hunched

over as he had been when lighting his pipe amid the thunderstorm, but now his hand moved rapidly from his forehead to his belly and then from pectoral to pectoral. He was crossing himself like priests do, except he kept doing it. Frantically.

"Someone took scary pills," Lindsay whispered.

As if hearing her, the burner fixed a wide-eyed, crazy-ass stare on Lindsay. His lips were moving, but he was too far away for Lindsay to hear what he said. In fact, she got the impression he wasn't really talking, just moving his lips in silent prayer. He lifted his hands toward her, palms out as if to stop an attacker. Deep cuts on his palms, still bleeding, formed the shape of crosses.

"They're real!" the boy suddenly shouted. "God protect us. They're real."

Lindsay jumped with fright and backed away. Even though she knew the kid was tripping hard and ugly, his cry terrified her. She didn't need this level of crazy in her life. So she ran off, his shouts following her through the crowd.

Once she was too far down the walk to hear the burner's shouts, Lindsay relaxed. She stopped walking and looked around at the shops and the crowd.

A little boy holding a dripping ice-cream cone stubbed his toe on the walkway in front of her and tumbled forward. Lindsay gasped and reached low, totally out of reflex. She caught the boy before he hit the boardwalk, but his ice-cream cone flew through the railing and into the sand. He looked around, confused for a moment, and then started to cry.

"Hey," Lindsay said, feeling bad for the kid. "Hey, it's okay. We'll get you another one."

The teary-eyed boy looked at her like she had a bug on her face. Then he started crying again.

Oh great, Lindsay thought. *What am I supposed to do now?*

"Are your parents here?" she asked.

Just then a shrill female voice rose up over Lindsay's shoulder. "Randy!"

She turned to see a girl stomping over the boards toward her. The girl had long platinum blond hair, perfectly flat and straight, hanging long enough to drape over the brightly colored bikini top she wore. Her skin was almond brown, and so uniform in color, Lindsay imagined she had the tan sprayed on recently.

"I'm sorry," the girl said, reaching down to grab

the little boy's hand. "He's such a total pain." She turned to the boy and said, "Randy. Don't go running off. Gah, it's like I've told you a billion times."

"Ice cream," the little boy said.

"It fell in the sand," Lindsay explained to the girl.

"Figures. That's like the third time this week."

"Is he your brother?"

"Sadly," the girl replied. She shook her head and waved a finger at him. She did it so dramatically Lindsay knew she wasn't really mad. "I'm Ev, and this is Randy."

"I'm Lindsay."

"Cool. Who are you here with?"

"Parents."

"Noooooo," Ev cried, so loudly a bunch of tourists turned to look. She broke up laughing and made an exaggerated expression of shock. "That's like the worst. I mean, my parents are here . . . someplace . . . but I'm totally avoiding them. Unfortunately, my freedom comes with a price: Randy."

"Ice cream," the boy whimpered.

"Yeah," Ev said. "We'll get you another ice cream, but you have to sit down and eat it this time."

Ev grabbed her brother's hand and gave him a playful yank. "Where you headed?" she asked Lindsay.

"Just hanging out."

"Well, come hang with us. We're in the Hot Dog back there. Smoothies are on me."

Lindsay only needed a second to say "Sure." Ev seemed like fun. Maybe a little wired, but still cool.

The Hot Dog was a gleaming tile and chrome café with a long neon sign in the shape of a hot dog behind the bar. Other neon tubes were shaped like waves and surfboards. The tiles were salmon pink and the tables matched.

Lindsay followed Ev and Randy into the cool interior. All of the tables were crammed with families, couples, and groups of friends. Ev raised her hand, waved to someone in the back of the room, and shouted, "Got him!" She seemed totally oblivious of the fact that the room was full of strangers.

At the back, two small tables had been pushed together, and three girls waved excitedly. Every one of the girls had straight platinum hair, a bikini top, white shorts, and a perfect tan. It was like they'd been to a cloning clinic or something.

"My entourage," Ev said to Lindsay. "It's so weird."

Lindsay smiled, not sure what to make of the strange group of girls.

After shoving Randy into the booth, Ev pulled back a chair and sat down. She introduced Lindsay to her friends. They all had fractured names: Char, Mel, and Tee.

Char, the girl on Lindsay's far left, had round cheeks and plump lips and wore a little too much makeup. Next to her sat Mel. Though the prettiest of Ev's entourage, Mel's outfit looked the most tragic. Her bikini top was old, the color faded, and her shorts were frayed at the legs. Her bleach job wasn't terribly fresh either, as dark roots nearly half an inch long ran from her scalp. The last girl, Tee, was small boned with green eyes that made her look like a cat. Though all of the girls smiled, their eyes were clouded with suspicion. Lindsay could tell that Char liked her least of all.

Lindsay felt uncomfortable, but Ev said, "So Lindsay here saved Randy's life."

The girls gasped.

"Totally true," Ev continued. "The little creep about fell off the boardwalk and snapped his neck.

Then Supergirl showed up and saved him. She rocks. Be nice."

Before Lindsay knew what was happening, the girls were leaving their seats and swarming her, hugging her. "My god, you could've been killed," one, maybe Mel, whispered. Lindsay nearly laughed at all the overblown drama, but she decided to play it cool.

It turned out that Ev was something of a local celebrity. Or at least she used to be a local who would soon be a celebrity. Knowing from a very young age that Redlands Beach and its surrounding areas were not for her, Ev pursued her dreams. Last year she'd asked her parents to let her go to New York to stay with a cousin, so she could break into modeling and acting. Already she'd done a number of ads for national magazines and was offered a small part in an independent film.

"I'm just like hanging with the old school until I have to start shooting," Ev explained. "We've hung out since we were like four or something. Once I started getting work, my girls here got all *Single White Female* on me. Have you seen that movie? No? It's awesome. But anyway, it's just a goof. Mel is already letting hers grow out."

Lindsay didn't know what to say. She found her-self suddenly intimidated by Ev. A model? An actress? Kate was never going to believe this.

"What about you?" Ev asked. "You're like here with your parents. Are you on a leash or can you cut loose?"

"I'm here, aren't I?" Lindsay replied. "I cut the leash a long time ago."

"Exssssssssssellent," Ev said, rubbing her hands together.

"Totally." "Awesome." "Cool." Ev's entourage chimed in.

"So," Ev said. "Here's the schedule. We'll be on the beach at like ten A.M. every morning, because morning sun isn't as harsh on the skin. Around lunch, we hang here or over at the Java Pit, so we can plan our world domination. Afternoons, we totally relax, right? Mannies. Peddies. Facials. Whatever. At night we do the bonfire thing. I'm only in for the next four days, so join the carnival before it leaves town. Know what I'm saying?"

"Sure," Lindsay said, excited to know she wouldn't be totally dependent on her parents for entertainment.

And there's always Mark.

She wanted to see him again. Something about him touched her. Maybe it was the fact that he seemed trapped, and she wanted to help. Maybe it was just his bod. She didn't know, but she hoped their first conversation wouldn't be the last.

"Add another name to the VIP list," Ev said, wrapping an arm around Lindsay's shoulders. "Girl's got a full-access pass."

Lindsay smiled and leaned into Ev's hug.

This was going to be a very cool vacation after all.

At night we do the bonfire thing.

The bonfire was a tradition with Redlands Beach teens that went back generations. There on the beach, they built a cone of wood and lit it up, allowing the flames to illuminate their parties, giving each gathering a sense of celebration. Not that there was much to celebrate in Redlands Beach, not for teenagers anyway. Though most kids dreamed of getting out of town and leaving it all behind, few ever made it. Those that did often traded Redlands Beach for a town just like it. Against such a gloomy background, any star, even one as small as Ev, shined brightly.

The ocean roared on her right as Lindsay

picked her way over the sand toward the dancing flames in the distance. She didn't even know if this was the bonfire Ev meant, as she didn't get specific directions. In fact, Ev only said, "You totally can't miss us. We're like full-on tribal."

Her parents were thrilled to hear that she'd made friends already. Her mother gave her an I-told-you-so look, and her dad just looked pleased, like he'd introduced her to Ev and the other girls with fractured names. *Whatever,* Lindsay thought. She was happy, and they were happy, so it didn't really matter.

Or at least, she was mostly happy. Poor Mark. All cooped up in his room. She'd walked through the alley between the houses when she left, but his window was covered by a black shade, so she didn't see him. She thought about tapping lightly on the glass, maybe asking him to sneak out, but she didn't know him (or his guardians) well enough to try a stunt like that.

And of course, there was Kate's party. Lindsay called to check in on Kate after dinner. She could hear how nervous her friend was, even though Kate tried to play it cool. Fortunately Trey was there, helping Kate set up, keeping her distracted with jokes.

For a minute Lindsay was pissed off at her parents again. Hearing Kate on the edge of panic hurt, because Lindsay was too far away to do anything about it. Plus, there was the party itself. All of the fun. All of her friends. She should have been there, not here on some beach with a bunch of strangers.

After another ten minutes, Lindsay found herself at the edge of the bonfire's light. A stack of wood that came up to her waist burned and crackled. All around the flames, two dozen kids, boys and girls, sat in the sand. Some drank from beer cans, others upended bottles of cheap whiskey and vodka. A Shakira song blasted from a portable player, seemed to stoke the fire with a dense bass beat.

Ev's laugh, like a siren, drew Lindsay to the far side of the fire. The girl and her friends were all giggling wildly, rocking forward with the power of their own amusement. Around them, a group of boys, some in nice shorts and others in ragged cutoffs, sat listening and smiling.

"Totally!" Ev cried amid a splutter of shrill giggles. "He's like Rob Schneider, only creepier. And he was like trying to French me, like 'eat my tongue,' ahhhhhh." She waved her hands in the air as if fighting off the boy she was describing. Tears were filling her eyes, she found the moment so funny. "And I'm all, noooooooooooooo!"

The kids around the fire broke up laughing.

"Supergirl," Ev shouted, her voice slurring.

"Hey," Lindsay said.

"Pull up a boy and get comfortable."

A second later someone handed her a beer. She turned to thank whoever had given it to her. A guy with light brown hair smiled down at her. At first glance he was cute, but as Lindsay looked at him, she realized he was older than most of the kids around the fire. A lot older. Maybe twenty-three or twenty-four. Lindsay also noticed his teeth were kind of crooked, which made his smile look sinister. He worked out though. His pecs were huge and his arms were feathered with thick veins. She had to admit the guy had a nice body, but Lindsay preferred tighter bodies like Mark's.

"Thanks," she said.

"Anytime," he replied, his voice heavy with flirtation.

"That's Doyle," Ev called. "He has a lot to offer a girl. Know what I mean?" This sent Ev into another round of hysterics. Lindsay noticed she was already drunk.

Next to her, Ev's entourage said, "Totally," "A lot!", and "So much to offer."

Lindsay decoded the less-than-subtle message, and felt uncomfortable. She sipped at her beer. Doyle just kept smiling, nodding his head as if she'd already agreed to date him.

"Well, thanks," Lindsay said, then knelt on the sand to join in Ev's conversation.

Char slid closer to Ev until their butts touched and put an arm around her friend as if protecting her.

"So, Lindsay, do you have a boy back in Pittsburgh?" Tee asked. Her green eyes reflected the fire and they glowed like emeralds.

"Helensburgh," Lindsay corrected.

"Like there's any difference," Char said. She burst out laughing, but since no one else did, she reeled it in fast.

"Ease up on the meds, Char," Mel said. Lindsay looked her way.

"She's always trying to be funny, and it some-how continues to elude her," Ev added.

"Man, Ev," Char said, pouting.

"So, do you have a boy, or what?" Tee asked again. She flipped her hair over an ear and leaned toward Lindsay. It was obviously information she really wanted.

"No," Lindsay replied, though she thought about Mark. "No boy at home."

"Why not?"

"I don't know. I've gone out with a couple guys."

"You weren't in love?"

"Third degree much?" Ev interrupted. She took a long drink of beer and tossed the can in the sand. "Tee is a total perv. She wants like all of these private details."

"I do not!" Tee protested loudly. "Why are you being such a bitch tonight?"

"Because it's free and it's low-carb."

Doyle plopped down in the sand on the other side of Lindsay and flashed her a smile. She crossed her arms over her knees.

"Doyle," Ev said, "why don't you get me another beer?"

"I just sat down."

"Think of it as exercise."

Doyle looked around smiling and nodding his

head until he realized Ev was serious. He shook his head and whispered a curse under his breath. Then he stood and showered sand down on Lindsay's head before stomping off.

Lindsay noticed that the sand had also fallen on the lip of her beer can, so she set it down. She ran her hands through her hair to get rid of the grit there and noticed Char giving her a nasty look.

She's jealous, Lindsay thought. *But is she jealous of Doyle or Ev? Maybe both?*

"Sorry about Doyle," Ev said. "He's like a hound with a scent. Let's take a walk."

Lindsay and Ev stood. A moment later the other girls were also standing up, brushing sand off their backsides. Mel paused to check a tear over the pocket of her white shorts. She fussed with the edges, looking sad. Doyle appeared with Ev's beer. She took it from him and said, "Thanks, baby," before taking a deep drink. Doyle turned his attention back to Lindsay.

"Where are we going?" Char asked.

"Lindsay and I are going to wander for a few." Char's face fell. Anger crept into her expression. "I want to give the new girl the deluxe tour."

Once they were north of the bonfire, out of

earshot of the others, Ev slowed her pace. She drank from her beer and looked at Lindsay.

"Sorry about Doyle. He's always around. The inland girls usually like him."

"He's kind of old."

"Yeah," Ev replied with a laugh. "He is, I guess, but he'll always be around, like the ocean and the sand."

"He's just part of the scene?"

"Totally. And the scene never changes. That's why I hate it here."

"It seems cool enough," Lindsay said. She was trying to be nice. She didn't really know what to think about it.

"Yeah," Ev said. "It's cool if you like quicksand."

"Quicksand?"

"You know, in those movies where people get stuck in it, and they struggle, and it sucks them down faster? That's what Redlands is like. Mel and Tee are already up to their necks in it. They'll both meet boys and get jobs at some grocery store or restaurant and have a bunch of kids. It's like already written in stone. Char's got a little time yet."

Lindsay hadn't expected this burst of philosophy. She didn't think Ev was particularly deep, what with all her party girl talk and loud attitude.

"I've been planning to get out since I was a kid," the platinum blonde continued. "I just knew I couldn't stay here. So I got my GED and I worked at that crappy Dairy Queen on Harper's and I bailed, because I knew I had to pull myself out. My girls aren't like me, though. They think they can wait and something will happen or someone will come along and save them. The problem is, they think I'm the one who can save them now."

"Don't you want to help them?"

Ev stopped walking. The night breeze ruffled her straight hair, blew it across her face. She pushed it back with her hand. "I can't," she said. "They're a part of this place, just like Doyle. They're deep in the quicksand, and if I try to pull them out, they'll drag me back in. My manager totally helped me see that."

Now Lindsay understood. Ev was just quoting something an adult had told her. She hadn't created the words, but she certainly believed in them. This left Lindsay shaken. Ev seemed harder to her now. Colder. How could she not want to help her friends?

"You could talk to them," Lindsay offered. "Maybe

they'd realize there was more out there."

"All we did when we were little girls was talk about getting away from here. I did it, but they're afraid to even try. The fact is, some people just can't be saved."

Lindsay didn't want to believe that.

Lindsay lay in bed, staring at the ceiling. The party had been fun, she guessed. By the time she and Ev got back, most everyone was wasted. She didn't know anyone and didn't know what to expect from them, so she kept quiet, just sipping at her beer, never letting herself totally relax. Seeing Ev's entourage after their chat totally depressed her. They seemed like blind prisoners—trapped but unable to see the bars around them. *The fact is, some people just can't be saved.* The older guy, Doyle, followed her around, always smiling, always nodding his head like he was agreeing with things she hadn't said. When he spoke, it was always some lame double entendre meant to sound charming or cool. At a little past midnight, Lindsay decided to bail.

Now she stared at the ceiling. Kate's party would be in full swing. Lindsay would have known a lot of people. She could have relaxed, and Doyle would have been a thousand miles away, nodding at some other girl.

For the second night in a row, she heard the odd chanting, the chimes, and the drum. This was another oddity. If Mark's guardians were so hung up on New Age crap, how could they be so strict? So mean?

She pictured them. Muscular. Severe. Nasty. Playing lousy music into the middle of the night just to torment Mark.

"I'm hating this," Lindsay said to her ceiling.

The chanting grew quieter. The drums beat louder.

"Crap."

Lindsay climbed out of bed. She went to the window and looked into the sandy alley below. A frame of light surrounded a black shade behind Mark's window. The lines of light seemed to fade and brighten with shadowy movement. Maybe he was watching TV.

But she didn't remember seeing a TV in his room.

She leaned away from the window. Knowing she'd never get to sleep, Lindsay dressed herself in shorts and a salmon-colored blouse, which she buttoned slowly. She slipped on a pair of flip-flops and left the room. Her ears were still alert, trying to pick up any revealing sound from the house next door.

In the kitchen she grabbed a diet cola from the refrigerator and walked to the porch.

Lindsay sat on the wooden bench, cradling the soda can in her lap. Dark water stretched to the horizon, where it met the sky. Both were black, but of different depth. The ocean was as dark as onyx. The sky was more of a plum black pierced by millions of tiny stars. She watched the ghostly white lines of foam crest and fall to the beach and listened to the rhythmic crash of the waves. She breathed in the salty air. Sipped from her drink.

To the north, Ev's bonfire party was probably still going on, with everyone paired off. Maybe tomorrow night Lindsay would loosen up a bit more, have a better time.

She began to relax, letting the sound of the surf lull her. She thought about Mark, thought about what hanging out with him would be like. Not hanging out like they did that afternoon, with a windowsill separating them, but really hanging out. Going for coffee or lying on the beach. She wished Mark were with her now, sharing the bench and the cool night air.

But would she get the chance to spend any normal time with him? She was only staying at her uncle's place for nine more days. What if Mark was grounded the whole time and they only got to chat with a wall between them? That would be a major shame. Even though it had a *Romeo and Juliet* flavor, that kind of romance was completely unfortunate.

She glanced at the house next door and was surprised to see movement on the porch. Her heart tripped rapidly. For a moment, she felt certain Mark was sneaking out.

Please, let it be him.

She squinted, trying to make sense of the shadow on the neighboring porch. Leaning close to the side railing, she was about to whisper Mark's name, but paused. She was glad she did.

The shape was too broad and short to be Mark. It seemed to glide across the porch like a black ghost until it emerged into the moonlight.

Lindsay's breath caught in her throat. Wearing the same slicker he'd worn the first time she saw him, Jack, the more muscular of Mark's guardians, descended the stairs. His feet sank into the sand, and he paused, staring out at the ocean. The slicker flapped against him in the breeze coming off the water. Lindsay pulled away from the railing, pushed herself tight to the bench. She held her breath, frightened she might be discovered.

She didn't want Jack to know she was there. He scared her. Both of Mark's guardians did.

Finally the stubby man left his place by the stairs. He walked across the sand toward the surf. When he reached the tide's edge, he removed the slicker, and Lindsay saw he wore a loose, boxy bathing suit. Black, of course. Across the man's back were numerous dark lines: a tattoo. Lindsay couldn't tell what the design was (or if it was several individual patterns), but it covered his entire back.

So much for being a respectable authority figure.

Jack dropped the slicker on the sand and ran into the surf. Water crashed against his shins. He dove forward, disappearing beneath a white curtain of froth.

"I hope you drown," she mumbled. "Or sharks

chew off your legs."

For a moment, she thought her wish had been granted. She searched the ocean for any sign of the man, but he seemed to have vanished into the waves. *Is he some kind of fish-man? A sea creature that can make itself look human?*

That's stupid. But where did he go?

The explanation was simple enough: It was too dark for her to see. Still, Jack's disappearance creeped her out.

Lindsay decided to go inside and put a locked door between herself and the freak. She stood, but a second later a sharp click sounded in the night. She turned quickly to the source of the noise.

On the porch of the house next door, a tiny flame flickered. In its dancing light, she saw the face of Mark's other guardian, Doug. The tall, bald man was lighting a cigarette, and he was looking right at her.

Terrified, Lindsay raced inside.

The Redlands Mobile Home Park was half a mile south of the house Lindsay's uncle owned. Farther south, rocky outcroppings broke the beach with jagged black ridges, jutting out into the frothing surf. In the early morning hours, a white Jeep owned by the Redlands Beach Patrol rolled over the sand in this area, doing a nightly sweep. Sometimes they caught teens making out, drinking, or carrying on so loudly the patrol was forced to run them off. Often enough, they found nothing.

Tonight was terribly different though. As the Jeep approached the shore, its headlights fell on what one of the patrolmen initially thought was a pile of wet clothes. It only took him a few seconds to see the arms poking out from beneath the soaked fabric, and what he'd mistaken for a damp woolen sweater was actually a knot of thick knotted hair, covering the head of a young man. Always hopeful, the patrolman considered the possibility that this young man had fallen asleep on the beach, and was perhaps too drunk to notice the tide coming in to douse him. He finally accepted the dreadful truth when he noticed a group of crabs climbing over the boy's bare legs and feet like large armored spiders, already at work on him with their pincers.

The patrolman parked close and leaped from his Jeep. He ran to the body and shooed away the horrible crabs. He reached down for the boy's arm, lifted it, checking the wrist for a pulse, but found none. That was when he noticed the cross carved into the boy's palm.

In the morning, again woken by bright sunshine, Lindsay dashed from her bed to the window seat. She couldn't help herself. She looked down into the yard, scoping the sand to see if one or both of Mark's guardians were there. They weren't. She looked at his window, and her heart sank. The black shade was still drawn behind the glass.

"We're going to the beach this morning," her dad said when Lindsay went downstairs for her coffee. "Gonna stake out a good place before all the riffraff take over the shore. You interested?"

"Maybe," Lindsay said. "I promised Ev I'd hang with her this morning. But I think she might be hurting today. We'll see."

"Sure, honey," her dad said, his Winnie the Pooh happy-face changing to a look of concern.

In her room, Lindsay took her coffee to the window seat. The shade was still drawn over Mark's window. She thought about calling Kate. Talking about Mark might be a sufficient substitute for seeing him, but it was way too early, especially if her friend's party had been a success.

Where is he?

Lindsay opened her laptop and powered it up, casting quick glances at the house next door as she waited for the machine to boot. She sipped her coffee and heard her parents moving around in the hall at the top of the staircase.

She settled in to read through emails when her

dad knocked on the bedroom door. He waited for her to say "Come in," before poking his head in the room.

"Just want to make sure you've got everything you need before we head out."

"I'm fine, Dad."

"Oh, and I want you to be careful if you decide to go swimming. A young man drowned last night."

"You're kidding?" Lindsay said, horrified. "Here?"

"Down the beach by the rocks," her dad replied. "The news made it sound like he was some kind of druggie, and he just got caught in an undercurrent or something. Couldn't fight it because he was high. Anyway, just be careful."

"I wasn't planning on swimming anyway. But thanks. You and Mom have a good time."

"Well, we'll have your mom's cell."

"Dad," Lindsay said, smiling and shaking her head. "It's not like you're going to Canada or anything. The beach is like five feet away."

"I just thought that if you changed your mind, it'd be easier to find us."

"Easier than stepping out on the porch and

looking for the biggest dork on the beach?" she asked, just joking.

"Hey," her dad said. "You shouldn't talk about your mom that way."

"You can leave now," Lindsay said with a laugh.

Alone in the room, Lindsay felt a pleasant kind of sadness. She knew this feeling had a name but couldn't remember what it was called.

As she glanced out at the house next door, she remembered her childhood visits to the beach. Back then the vacations were exciting. Despite her uncle's noisy friends and his smell, she really liked the family trips. In the mornings they all sat around the table and ate a big breakfast of pancakes or eggs with tons of sausage or bacon and lots of English muffins just waiting for gobs of jelly. Pleasantly stuffed, she went with her parents to the beach and played in the sand and surf, building little fat castles and digging ditches to create medieval landscapes for her dolls to roam. In the afternoon her parents would take her shopping or to a movie at the theater in town. And every night, just around sunset, while her mom and her uncle cleaned up the dinner dishes, her dad took her hand and led her back to the beach, right up to the shoreline to collect shells and pretty rocks. Once she'd had boxes of the souvenirs tucked under her bed at home.

She tossed most of those out last year, except for three really cool shells that sat on her bedroom windowsill. Like her anticipation of the vacations, her interest in the souvenirs had faded.

Already this morning, she'd received six emails from Kate, three from Trey, and several from other friends. Apparently, Kate's party had turned into a full-on crisis. Four of the popular boys from school, including Nick Faherty and his brother, got so drunk they were puking in the kitchen sink. Kate got into a big fight with Constance Turner, who was making out with Chad Olivieri on Kate's bed. Of course, Kate liked Chad, so that made it blow all the more. Matt broke a lamp—"which is totally irreplaceable"—and Funkster, Kate's terrier, got out and disappeared until morning. The police even showed up because the Jacksons next door complained about the noise. In later emails, Kate wanted to know where Lindsay was and why her cell phone was turned off: "I so need to talk to you!!!"

Trey reported on the party as well. He thought it was the coolest party *EVARRRR*! But of course, he didn't have to clean up the house or endure the wrath of Kate's parents.

Lindsay looked away from her computer, and her heart beat faster. Kate and her party were forgotten.

The shade was up in Mark's room. He stood in the window, looking at her.

Waiting for Mark's guardians to leave was like teetering on the edge of a cliff. She busied herself with emails and spent thirty minutes putting different outfits together on the bed. It was nearly an hour after first seeing Mark in his window before Lindsay heard the car next door pull out.

Excited, she ran downstairs and out the front door. In the alley of sand between the two houses, she slowed her pace and smoothed down the fabric of her blouse.

At Mark's window, she noticed the strange metal corner pieces driven into the wood again. This time, she touched one out of curiosity. It felt ice-cold to the touch, despite the fact it had to be ninety degrees outside.

"Hi," Mark said. He still wore the distressed jeans and the black shirt that hung loose from his shoulders.

"Hey," Lindsay said. "How's it going?"

Mark shrugged. "Sorry about yesterday," he told her. "I feel like a total geek for freaking out that way."

"They're really strict, huh?"

"You can't imagine," Mark said. His face changed, and he looked happy. "You look really nice today."

"Thanks. So do you."

"No, I don't," he said. "Don't have any clothes that fit me here."

"I hate everything I brought," Lindsay said.

"How's your vacation so far?" Mark asked.

"It's okay. I met some kids yesterday. They're cool, I guess."

"If I could get out of here, I'd make sure you had a good trip."

"Oh really?" Lindsay said a bit too loudly. She got her voice under control and said, "What would we do?"

"I don't know. I'd teach you how to surf. You said you wanted to learn. Then we could find a nice place for dinner, and after that walk on the beach for a couple of hours. We could build a fire and talk and stuff."

"That sounds great," she said.

"Yeah. Right now, anything sounds great to me as long as it doesn't involve Doug, Jack, or this damn room."

"Why don't you come out here?" she asked. "Maybe we could talk out back. You'd totally make it inside before they found out."

Mark looked at her like she had just sprouted a snout. His eyebrows scrunched and his head turned to the side like a curious dog.

"Can't," he said. "It's like, the window. But maybe you could come in?"

Before she knew it, she was climbing over the sill. Once her shoulders were well into the room, Mark grabbed her gently and pulled her the rest of the way. She glided over his desk and felt how strong he was.

"There," he said. "That's better."

The first thing that struck Lindsay about Mark's room was how stark it seemed. Outside she'd noticed the lack of wall decorations and the minimal furnishings, but standing in the room made her feel the emptiness of the place. It could have been the tidiness. The pile of clothes she'd noticed yesterday against the closet door was gone, leaving the floor spotless. Mark's bed was made, blankets smoothed down tight and flawless. The desk by the window, a simple wooden top with narrow legs, looked brand-new, as if it had never been used. No papers littered the surface. No scratches marred the wood. To her left was an open door, leading to a bathroom, and against the same wall as the window was the piano she'd noticed before.

"Do you play?" Lindsay asked.

"Sure," Mark said. He crossed to the piano and lifted the cover off the keys. He hit a key with his index finger and the note chimed crisply. "Well, I used to. I haven't felt much like it lately." He sat down on the bench. "Any requests?"

"I don't know much piano music," Lindsay admitted, feeling foolish.

"Hmm." Mark stared at the keyboard for a moment, and then his fingers came down on the keys.

The music that followed was classical, Lindsay knew, but she didn't know the piece or the composer. Still, to her it sounded amazing. Each note and chord meshed together in a beautiful weave of sound. But it also sounded kind of sad.

Mark stopped after a couple of minutes and said, "Chopin."

"What?"

"The piece is by Chopin."

He returned his attention to the piano and started banging out a high tempo piece that sounded like old-time rock and roll. This only kept his attention for a minute though. "And that was Jerry Lee Lewis."

"You play really well."

"Thanks." The compliment seemed to brighten Mark up a lot. He played a few more snippets, identifying each artist when he finished. "The Beatles." "Elton John." "Linkin Park."

The only song Lindsay knew was the last one. She liked it a lot, and though she didn't know the others, she liked them, too, but probably only because Mark had chosen to play them.

And there she stood, in Mark's room. Alone with him. Her thoughts raced and collided, leaving her without anything to say. She supposed she could comment on the room or something. It wasn't so bad. It felt a little chilly to her, but it was okay. Still, it was no place to spend your summer.

"You're shaking," Mark said, rising from the piano bench.

"Too much AC," she replied, hugging herself.

"Do you want another shirt or something? Doug and Jack keep the place like a refrigerator most of the time. I guess I'm just used to it now."

"No, I'm fine," Lindsay assured him.

"Do you want to sit down?" Mark asked, indicating the desk chair behind her. "You might be warmer if you stay by the window."

"Thanks."

"I'd offer you something to drink, but I think Doug or Jack might notice."

"Don't worry about it," Lindsay said.

Then they fell silent. Lindsay sat in the desk chair, found it comfortable. Mark stood in the middle of the room, looking a little shy and uncertain. She could have just looked at him for an hour, but it was totally weird not saying anything. It made her tremble more.

"I like your room."

"Thank you. It'd be okay if I could get out of it every now and then."

"Well, they can't keep you locked up forever. How long are you grounded?"

"Forever," he said with a smile. "It's really complicated. And they're going to be back soon."

Lindsay watched the sad expression leak over Mark's face. She again wondered if his guardians hit him, and the thought made her chest hurt.

"Are you okay?" she asked. "I mean, they aren't hurting you, are they? Because that's totally illegal."

"You can't get involved," Mark said sharply. "It's not what you think."

"It just seems so unfair."

"Look, Lindsay," Mark said, turning his head a bit as if looking for spies in his nearly empty room. "If I tell you something, will you promise not to tell anyone else? I'm serious. You *can't* tell anyone. Not your friends or your parents or anyone!"

Thrilled that he was going to share a secret with her, Lindsay leaned closer. She put her hands on her knees and nodded her head.

"I swear."

Again Mark looked around his room. "I can't explain it all, because there's not enough time. But you know how sometimes the government will take people who know things and hide them, move them to another part of the country, change their names?"

"Sure," Lindsay said. She saw it all the time on television.

"Well, it's like that," Mark said. "But it's not *just* that. I think something's wrong. I'm not supposed to be a prisoner. I mean, they never made it sound that way before, but I can't get out of this house. The doors are locked, and they've got alarms. They've got this stuff they put on the windows and doors, and if I touch them it leaves a mark. That's why you have to open the window for me. The worst part is, I couldn't leave if I wanted to. Because even though these guys are bad, there are a lot worse things out there looking for me. So I can't go to the cops or call my friends, because if anyone finds me, I'm toast."

"I don't believe this," Lindsay said.

It was just an expression. She totally believed it. If Mark were a liar with strict parents, he could climb through the window and run away. He had to seriously believe he was in danger, or he wouldn't just stay inside taking their abuse.

"What happened?" she asked.

"It has to do with my father," Mark said. "You might say he's involved with the underworld. Anyway, he got me involved in some things that are totally out of my control."

On the trip out to her uncle's house, Lindsay had felt like a prisoner, kidnapped by her parents and dragged away from her life. Now she saw how silly that was. Mark *was* a prisoner, a real one.

"Is there anything I can do?"

"No," he said. "I mean, I like seeing you. I really do. It's been a long time since I met anyone even remotely normal. So if you want to visit and talk and stuff, that's cool, but you really can't get involved. If the muscle thugs found out, you could get into real trouble."

"They can't do anything to me," Lindsay said.

"They can," Mark said sadly. "They can, and they will if they find out. You don't know them. They're capable of things you can't even imagine."

"Well maybe . . . ," Lindsay began.

"Oh, crap! I'm so sorry!"

The voice startled them both. Mark leaped back toward his bed, and Lindsay spun in the desk chair, her heart racing in her throat.

Ev stood at the window, her hands over her

111

mouth like she'd just witnessed something shocking. Again she wore a bikini top, this time white to show off her tan, and her hair was smooth and sleek like sheets of snowy satin.

"I swear I wasn't spying," Ev said quickly. "I just came by to walk you down to the beach, and no one was home at your place."

"It's cool," Lindsay said, though it wasn't.

"Hey," Mark said, not stepping closer to the window.

Lindsay checked his expression to see if he was all about Ev's look. She couldn't tell what he was thinking, but she knew well enough what her own thoughts were. She didn't want the model-actress here, competing with her for Mark.

I wouldn't stand a chance.

"Well, I'm so sorry," Ev said, exaggerating every syllable.

Turn off the drama, Lindsay thought. *Jeez, it's not like we were naked or something.*

"No problem," Mark said. "I was just telling Lindsay I had to get some things done." He looked quickly toward the door. "I really can't hang. Doug and Jack will be back soon."

Mark was being subtle, but Lindsay totally knew

what he was saying. He wanted her to get Ev away from the house before his guardians returned. It would be hard enough for Lindsay to slip out without being noticed; trying to drag Ev away without making a scene would be far harder. She nodded slightly, telling him she understood.

"Well, my tan isn't getting any darker in here," she said, quickly rising from the chair. Lindsay walked across the room to Mark and put her arms around him. She hugged him tightly. "See ya."

"Please don't bring Barbie back," Mark whispered in her ear.

Lindsay giggled and held him tighter, feeling his muscles through the loose black T-shirt. His arms wrapped around her in a secure embrace, and she didn't want to leave. But then he let her go.

"Later?" he asked, smiling at her.

"Later," she agreed. *Definitely*.

"So how hot is *he*!" Ev gushed as they walked over the sand.

"I know."

Already the beach was swarming with people. Men and women lay out on towels. Children chased the surf. Music from radios and CD players competed with the ocean's song.

It was a beautiful day. But Lindsay found herself wishing she were still in Mark's simple room.

"No wonder you were shooing Doyle away like a stray mutt, which he is by the way. He's fun, but he's a total hound, and in no way is he Mr. Yummy Butt. My god. Why didn't you tell me you had a boyfriend?"

"He's not my boyfriend," Lindsay said, blushing. "We just met."

"Well, you better snare that boy, Supergirl," Ev said excitedly. "Oh. Oh. Oh. You have *got* to bring him to the bon'."

"He's grounded." Lindsay's foot came down wrong on the sand, and she stumbled. The weight of her tote bag nearly pulled her to the beach. "Damn. Anyway, he's locked up for a few days. Total ass parents."

Even if he weren't grounded, Lindsay didn't like the idea of taking Mark to the bonfire. She wasn't ready to share him with anyone yet, especially Ev and her entourage.

And there they were. Twenty yards down the beach, three blondes—Mel and Tee and Char. They sat up simultaneously and waved. Lindsay could already hear them shouting to get Ev's attention.

"Gang's all here," Ev said, giggling and waving back.

Lindsay lay on her back, staring up at the silver-blue sky, her skin pleasantly warmed by the sun. Ev and the other girls chatted around her, and Kate cried in her ear. She'd been crying for the last thirty minutes. Lindsay adjusted the PDA against her cheek and listened while her friend vented.

". . . it was so gross. I mean, Nick is always so cool, and there he was spewing chunks in the sink, and Funkster was lost. I didn't know what to do. And that's *after* I caught Constance with Chad, so I already felt like crap and just wanted everyone to go home anyway. I about died when the police showed up, but Trey was there and he totally talked them down, but by then everything was so screwed up . . ."

Lindsay reached for her bottle of water and squirted some over her tongue. "So what's the actual damage? I know about the lamp. What else? Stains on the carpet? Cigarettes on the patio, the rug?"

"No, nothing like that, thank heavens."

"Okay, so you have to explain the lamp, and you need a backup story in case the Jacksons decide to tell your parents about the cops."

"My parents totally hate the Jacksons. They wouldn't talk to them."

"What about party supplies? Have you gotten rid of everything?"

"Trey's coming over later to help me with that junk. I would have died without him."

"So, did you piss anyone besides Constance off?" Lindsay asked.

"No," Kate said. "I don't think so. Trey really handled a lot of that stuff. He was just great. By the time everyone was spewing in the sink, I was locked in my room, crying."

"Well, Trey said it was a great party. He told me everyone was raving about it."

"Really?"

"Yes. You just couldn't enjoy it, because you were in the middle of it seeing all of the problems. Go to the school blog and see what people are saying."

"I couldn't."

"Just do it," Lindsay said. "They're probably already voting you homecoming queen. I've got to go."

"Oh," Kate muttered. "Okay. I'll go check the blog. Thanks, Linds."

"No prob. Call me later."

"I will."

Lindsay disconnected and sat up. The towel beneath her squished into the sand. She took off her sunglasses and surveyed the beach. It was near noon, and the shore was covered in sunbathers.

"Trauma at home?" Ev asked.

Lindsay looked at the girl, saw her staring out over the ocean as if she'd already heard the answer to her question and it bored her. "It's nothing," Lindsay said.

"I bet," Char said, falling back on her towel.

"Ignore her," Mel whispered in Lindsay's ear.

"Yeah," Tee agreed. "She's just jealous because Ev likes you. She's like threatened. She thinks now that Ev is famous, she's going to bail or something. But even when she's in New York, she's still with us, you know? She's a total friend, like you are with Kate."

"I know," Lindsay said, noticing the certainty in the girl's green eyes. She looked back in Ev's direction. The young model still watched the waves, seemingly indifferent to all around her.

When she looked back at Tee and Mel, she couldn't help but see them as victims, up to their neck in a quicksand pit, waiting and waiting for someone to pull them free.

The bonfire blazed, whipping over the sand with
the gusting wind. Ev seemed quieter tonight, less
buzzed, but her entourage was in full party down-
hill. Bottles drained. Beer cans emptied. Blunts
passed among the kids, who sat and stared in awe
at the flames. Tonight's bonfire was being dedicated to Lester Krohl. That was the name of the
kid that drowned last night. Apparently, he was a
full-on looz with a taste for weed and harder
drugs. When Ev and her crowd talked about
Lester, Lindsay couldn't help but realize he was the
burner she'd seen prowling outside Mark's house.
He'd totally scared her when she saw him again on

the boardwalk, but she still found his death disturbing.

Despite having the night dedicated to him, Lindsay got the distinct impression that Lester wasn't a well-liked boy. If anything, his death was being used as a hollow excuse for another night by the flames.

After hearing more than she wanted to about Lester Krohl, Lindsay stood a little away from the crowd, closer to the ocean, watching the tide crash in and slowly recede. She held a beer. She'd been at the party for an hour and it was still three quarters full. Doyle was prowling again. He'd arrived with a pretty girl, whom he was all but ignoring in favor of watching Lindsay.

She wished she'd just stayed at home. Over dinner with her parents, Lindsay felt uneasy. Restless. She could feel Mark in the house next door. He was so close to her. She wanted to talk to him. Wanted to have him hold her again. She wanted to help him.

You better snare that boy, Supergirl.

Yeah, right, Lindsay thought. They couldn't spend more than ten minutes together because of his guardians. They couldn't even talk on the phone or email. *Or can we?* She never thought to ask Mark if he had a cell. Didn't everybody? She figured Doug and Jack boosted it when Mark got grounded, but maybe they'd never allowed him to have one in the first place.

It's so unfair.

"Thinking about Yummy Butt?" Ev asked, draping her arm over Lindsay's shoulders.

"No," Lindsay lied. She added a laugh to show Ev how ridiculous her question was. "Just catching a buzz."

"Cool," Ev said, flipping her hair a little against the ocean breeze. "You totally can't like worry about him. Okay? Like he's hot and all, but he's also got to have some major issues. I mean, did you see that room? Like it's a total cell. So not normal."

You don't know what you're talking about.

"I know," Lindsay agreed. She sipped her beer. It was warm, but she drank it anyway.

"It's like you have to hang with the right people," Ev said. "Like I was saying last night. I worked too hard to get out of the dirt, and I'm not letting anyone pull me back. It's the same with that Mark guy. He's going to hold you back, and you've got to take care of *you*."

She didn't know what to think. Maybe Ev was right. But earlier in the day Ev was all "You have got to bring him to the bon'," and now the girl was telling her to break things off.

Like there was anything to break off.

"I'm here for you, Supergirl," Ev said. Then she walked back toward the fire.

Lindsay was a little drunk.

When Ev left, she'd finished her first beer in three gulps and then got another one. She didn't often drink, so by the time she held her second empty beer can, her head was light and the sand seemed particularly squishy. She danced with Tee and Mel for a bit. Char was kicked back in the sand talking to some boy with a shaved head and lime green shorts. Doyle kept insinuating himself between Lindsay and the girls, but she turned away, toward the fire, and let the music command her feet.

"You're driving me crazy," Doyle whispered in her ear as he attempted to grind his hips into her backside.

Lindsay spun away, laughing. "You were at crazy long before I got behind the wheel."

Doyle grabbed his stomach as if shot. "Ahhh," he groaned. "So mean."

Lindsay left him to his theatrics and wandered away from the fire.

"Hey," Tee called. "Where are you going? The party's like right here."

"Be right back," Lindsay called over her shoulder.

She trudged through the sand and eased her way through a group of kids at the fire's edge, working her way back to the cooler higher up on the beach. After opening a fresh one, she saw a pudgy guy in a brightly colored shirt, and since she was feeling a little flirty, she went up and started chatting with him. He introduced himself to her, but she didn't quite catch his name. It was Bart or Burt or something. His face was kind of round, and he reminded her way too much of her dad. He seemed really nice, though. Harmless anyway.

They talked for about fifteen minutes before Doyle decided to end the conversation. He danced forward and put his hands on Lindsay's hips, held her tightly so she couldn't get away again.

"You can let me go now."

"No," Doyle said. "I can't. You've been a part of me since we met."

Oh please, Lindsay thought. He was looking at her with sad puppy eyes, totally fake. Did this crap really work on other girls?

"Hey, Doyle," the pudgy kid said.

What's his name? Lindsay wondered. *Burt? Bart?*

"Move it, short round," Doyle said angrily. "You so don't want to get in the middle of this."

Lindsay tried to pull away, but his grip tightened. "Okay, Romeo, that's as far as this rolls."

"Come on, just a few minutes. We'll go someplace quiet. Have a beer."

Lindsay looked around for help. Bart or Burt just gazed at the sand, backing away. Mel and Tee were dancing with guys by the bon'. Char was ignoring the boy talking to her. She watched Lindsay's predicament, grinning from ear to ear with evil glee.

Doyle pushed in closer and slid his hand up Lindsay's waist, until his palm was suddenly cupping her left breast. That was it!

Lindsay stomped down hard on Doyle's foot. The sand gave a bit and she stumbled to the side, but she righted herself in time to get in a flat-handed blow to his nose before he recovered.

Doyle skittered back, making a wet snuffling noise. He tripped and landed on his ass.

Finally, something she'd learned in school paid off. She'd thought the self-defense class was a total waste of time, but it sure worked well enough on Doyle.

"Night," Lindsay said sharply. Then she walked away.

Her wrist hurt from striking Doyle, but Lindsay felt good. She'd spent a lot of the evening chatting with Mel and Tee. Both girls had tried so hard to be friendly, but she couldn't help but feel sorry for them. She didn't even know if she liked them or not. The pity got in the way. Mel was kind of quiet, but nice enough. Tee was more outgoing, but still subdued. Char just didn't like her, and Lindsay was fine with that. She knew the girl was jealous, though of all of Ev's entourage, she actually seemed to understand that Ev was going to leave them.

Lindsay approached her uncle's house, walking through the sand and smiling. When Mark's house came up on her right, butterflies erupted in her stomach.

Lindsay slowed as she reached the alley separating her uncle's house from Mark's. She glanced along the sandy trail and stopped dead. A block of ice dropped into her belly when she saw the girl creeping along the side of Mark's house.

Ev! The platinum hair, the bikini top. *That bitch.*

She crept along the side of the house toward the glowing light of Mark's window. He was still awake. The shade was up, and Ev was going to make her move. Lindsay felt so stupid. She'd almost believed all of Ev's "don't waste your time on him" stuff. She wanted Lindsay away from Mark because Ev wanted him for herself.

Lindsay thought about yelling at Ev to get away from the house and the window and the boy next door, but she stopped herself.

If Mark was the kind of guy she believed he was, he'd send Ev away.

Please don't bring Barbie back.

If he was just another classless hick like the boys at the bonfire, Lindsay wanted to know it.

Lindsay quietly hurried across the alley to her uncle's porch. She tiptoed over the deck and leaned against the siding, listening, praying Mark didn't flirt with Ev. Her heart was already aching to think he might invite her into his room.

But that didn't happen. A sharp gasp came up from the side of the house. It was followed by another sound. Shrill but controlled. Muffled and quiet. Lindsay inched forward, wanting to see what was going on.

Ev raced along the sand, looking desperate. Her platinum hair whipped from side to side, slapping her face and shoulders as she stumbled and righted herself. She tore out of the alley, the sound of stifled sobbing rising from her. Wild eyes shone over hands clasped tightly to keep the cries in her mouth.

Moments later, the door of Mark's house flew open and Doug, the leaner of the two guardians, charged out onto the porch. He jumped the stairs, hit the beach with a dull thud, and kept running, kicking up small clouds of sand as he sprinted along the shore. Lindsay watched the chase, her pulse thundering in her ears. Jack appeared a moment later. He similarly ran and jumped. He hit the sand and paused, looking up the beach. Doug stopped, too, forty yards away. He put his hands on his hips and just watched the girl's flight.

Far down the beach, Ev looked back at the guardians. She screamed, a piercing, terrible sound.

But she never stopped running.

What the hell is happening? Ev was terrified by something. Something she had seen in Mark's room?

Lindsay silently backed to the door. She didn't want to be caught by Doug or Jack. No way did she want in on that. She slipped inside the screen door, then locked the heavy wooden door behind her.

Heart fluttering, she raced up the stairs to her room. At the window seat she cautiously leaned forward to look down.

A black shade descended over Mark's window.

And Lindsay knew she was right, knew what drove Ev away in such a panic. Ev had seen Mark being punished. She'd crept to his house, hoping to hook up. She looked through his window and saw ... whatever it was Doug and Jack did to Mark. The sounds Ev made weren't loud, so there was no way the guardians could have heard her. No way.

They had to see her looking in, witnessing their abuse. Once she was seen, Ev freaked.

It must have been so awful.

They're capable of things you can't even imagine.

The next morning.

"Are you okay?" Lindsay asked through the open window. She hadn't even waited for Mark's invitation to open it. She had to speak to him.

"What are you doing here?" Mark whispered, his voice breaking with anxiety. "Doug and Jack are in the next room."

"You have to let me call someone for you. This isn't right."

"Lindsay, you can't get involved in this. I told you. Go home. We'll talk if they leave again."

"If?"

"Something happened last night. I'm not even sure what, but they're on red alert out there."

"I know," Lindsay said. "I saw it. Look, take this." She handed Mark her cell phone. "Hide it under the bed or something. I programmed my number into the first speed dial. I'll have my Treo. I can use that. You can call me anytime or call for help if you need to."

"I can't take this," Mark said, lifting the device toward the window.

But Lindsay wouldn't take it. "You have to," she told him. "I want to know you're okay."

Lindsay sat in the kitchen, staring at her coffee. Her PDA rested on the table in front of her. When her dad came in and said, "You're up early," Lindsay muttered, "Couldn't sleep." Her dad bent over and kissed her forehead, stroked her hair, then went to the coffeepot.

"Your mom will be down in a minute."

"Okay."

She watched her dad pouring milk into his coffee mug. Last night at dinner his face had been red from a day in the sun, but now it was brown, and he looked more like a bear than ever.

"What are your plans for today?" he asked. "Your new friends dragging you off again?"

"I don't think so." She hoped she never saw those creeps again.

"You're welcome to join us on the beach if you want. That is, if you won't be too embarrassed being seen with your parents?"

"Of course I'll be embarrassed," Lindsay said, trying to make a joke. Her heart wasn't in it, and it came off dry and nasty. So she added, "How could I NOT be?" This time she put in enough flare to her voice to get the playfulness across.

Her dad chuckled, but it was a courtesy laugh at best. "You okay, honey?"

No, she thought. "Fine," she said. "Just a little tired."

"Well, some sun will do you good."

Such simple answers to everything, Lindsay thought. According to her dad, a little sun, some sea air, and a piece of pie were all anyone needed to cope with anything. The world could be crumbling down, and he'd be there handing out beach towels and slices of Dutch apple to everyone, telling them not to panic.

What was she going to do? What could she do?

Nothing, a small voice said to her. *You can't do a damn thing.*

She rarely listened to this annoying voice. It was a downer, a shot of pessimism she just didn't need. For most of her life, she'd been able to fix things. Fixed them for herself. Fixed them for her friends. Even helped her parents every now and then. Why couldn't she fix this? Why wasn't there a simple answer? A plan to follow? Something?

After an hour on the beach, Lindsay decided to get something to drink and get out of the sun for a while. So she sat in the shade of her uncle's porch, sipping an iced tea. She could still see her parents, who were closer to the water. Her dad's belly rose and fell steadily as he napped with a baseball cap over his face. Her mom lay on her stomach, reading a paperback. The light trill of her Treo brought Lindsay out of her revery. She fumbled with the PDA and finally answered.

"Hey," Mark said, his voice quiet and sounding very far away.

"Hey."

"Can you hear me?"

"Sure," Lindsay replied.

"I have to be quiet. Doug went out for a while, but Jack's napping in the next room. I can hear him snoring. Sounds like a hog with asthma."

Lindsay laughed and threw a look at the porch of the neighboring house.

"So what are you doing?" Mark asked.

"Sitting on the porch, having some tea."

"Not out with Barbie?"

"After last night . . . I don't think so."

There was a brief silence on the line. "What happened last night?"

"You don't know?"

"Lindsay, I haven't been out of the house in a week. I'm a little out of the loop."

So she told him about seeing Ev between their houses, how she was sneaking up to his window. How she totally freaked at what she saw.

"Well, that explains a lot," Mark said. "I was in the living room, watching TV, when Doug and Jack went charging through like a couple of startled water buffalo. I didn't know what was going on, but the cops showed up in the middle of the night and really made a stink."

"The police were there?"

"Yeah. I thought Jack and Doug called them. I figured they caught someone trying to break in. I didn't know."

Lindsay felt awkward saying what she was about to say, but she had to. "I thought Ev might have seen them . . . you know . . . hurting you or something. She really looked scared."

"No. Nothing like that. They did send me back to my room though, like I was the one that did something wrong."

"What do you think she saw?" Lindsay asked.

"Don't know. Jack and Doug have done some really weird stuff. They perform these rituals sometimes. I don't know what they're trying to accomplish, but it can be pretty creepy to watch."

"Rituals?"

"Yeah. They're both totally into the occult. I've never seen them sacrifice a goat or anything, but they take it seriously. Like I said, some of that junk is just full-on creepy."

Suddenly Lindsay thought about the burner with the dreadlocks. He'd been on that side of the house, moving close to Mark's window. What if he'd seen the same thing as Ev?

They're real! God protect us. They're real.

"But why were they doing it in your room?"

"I don't know," Mark said. "But I'm kind of freaked out now. I mean, especially if your friend was all psych ward over it."

Lindsay didn't know what to say. The occult? She remembered the tattoos on Jack's back. Were they magic symbols? Some cult pattern?

"You know, Lindsay, it might be better if you took this phone back. If they find it on me, you could get into some real trouble, and I don't want that. Things have always been weird around here, but it feels like something is going to happen soon, something bad, and I don't want you to be hung up in it."

"No," Lindsay said. "You keep it. You might need it."

"I don't think it will help, but I do like chatting with you."

"Me, too."

For two days, Mark's guardians didn't leave the property, but he managed to find time—when they were outside or napping or watching TV in the next room—to call and quietly chat with Lindsay.

She was thrilled every time the Treo rang. Whether she was on the beach with her parents or in her room, IMing with Kate or Trey, she stopped everything to take his calls. Her parents commented several times on her good mood, and she did all that she could to assure them it was the vacation and nothing more. No way could she tell them about Mark.

And he was so great. He was funny and romantic, and one day, when Jack and Doug were out

137

tinkering with their car, Mark played another song for her on his piano. It was a simple tune, but really pretty. "It makes me think of you," he told her.

What wasn't so great were the calls she got from Tee and Mel. At first she didn't recognize the caller ID, so she let the calls go to her mailbox. When she retrieved the first one—from a Christie Molson—it took her a few seconds to realize it was Tee's voice. "Hey, Lindsay. Can you call me and Mel? It's like about Ev. We don't have cells, so just call my mom's. The number is . . ."

Lindsay didn't return the call. Or the next one, or the one after that. In fact, she erased the later messages without even listening to them. She so didn't care what Mel or Tee had to say about Ev. More than likely, they were just speaking *for* Ev, who wanted to feed Lindsay some story about what happened that night at Mark's. Whatever the case, she didn't trust Ev or her friends. Besides, she was enjoying her conversations with Mark and didn't want any annoying memories of the bonfire club interfering with it.

It was hard enough not being with him. So after he called late the second afternoon, she was happy. Mark sounded tired and upset, but his guardians were out, and he wanted to see her.

"What are these things?" Lindsay asked, running a finger over one of the metal corner pieces in the window frame.

Mark looked up from the piano, which he had been playing, and said, "Ugh. Doug and Jack have them all over the house. They picked them up at a magic shop years ago. They're supposed to keep out evil or something stupid. I think they just like the way they look. What do you think?"

"They're okay," Lindsay said. "I mean, they're small, so it's not like they're a total eyesore. I thought they might be part of an alarm or something."

"Nah, go ahead and wiggle one around. You'll see. No sirens."

Lindsay gave it a try. She grasped the metal. It was incredibly cold to the touch. Once she had the corner piece pinched between her thumb and forefinger, she gave it a tug.

It didn't budge.

"They're in really tight."

139

Mark stood from the piano bench and walked over to Lindsay. He put his arms around her waist, sending electric tingles up her spine. "Old-world craftsmanship," he said. He leaned down and nuzzled her hair. Then he kissed her neck.

She turned slowly and met his lips with her own. The kiss was hesitant and tender. But it was nice. He pulled away too soon.

"So, I wanted you to come over to tell you something," Mark said. He crossed the room and sat on the bed.

Lindsay joined him, sitting down with her hip touching his. "What is it?"

"I'm going to leave."

The news brought a thick nausea to her stomach. Her throat clenched tightly and her hands began to shake.

"W-when? Why?"

"Something is wrong here," he said. "Jack and Doug are losing it. The other day they took all of my clothes except what I'm wearing. I think they burned them. They're getting totally paranoid, and it's all coming down on me."

"But where will you go?" Lindsay asked.

"Doesn't matter. Anywhere but here. I'm only

telling you because I like you a lot, and if things weren't so screwed up, we might have . . ." He let the sentence trail away. He fell silent for a moment, then said, "The thing is, once I go, that's it. I can't come back. I can't see you anymore, and I can't call or anything. So, I guess this is kind of good-bye."

"Good-bye?" Lindsay felt incredibly ill. Never see each other again? "When are you leaving?"

"As soon as I can. I thought about taking off the minute Jack and Doug left, but I wanted to talk to you first, you know? I'm never sure when they'll leave or when they'll come back. It might be days before I get another chance, but I've got to get away from here. They're really scaring me now."

"Is there anything I can do?" Lindsay asked.

Mark pulled the cell phone from his pocket and handed it to her. It felt like a hot lump of coal in her hand. "You've already done enough."

She tried kissing him again, but he pulled away, shaking his head. "It'll only make things worse."

He stood and walked back to the piano. Solemnly, he sat down and began to play.

As far as Lindsay was concerned, it couldn't get any worse than this.

The first time Lindsay got into real trouble she was nine years old. One day after school, Kate talked her into smoking a cigarette. They were in Lindsay's room watching television, and the babysitter, Mrs. Kharn, was napping on the sofa downstairs. Kate produced the Marlboro and a book of matches, and though Lindsay's first response was "No way," a minute later she was drawing the nasty smoke into her throat. She only managed to take two puffs before feeling totally high—her head was spinning and light as air. They flushed the evidence down the toilet and swore to each other that they'd never touch another cigarette. Kate went home, and Lindsay brushed her teeth twice to get rid of the gross taste in her mouth.

To her mind, she had gotten away with it. It was an exciting feeling, like having the dual thrills of completing a dare and holding a secret all rolled up in one.

But she didn't get away with anything. Her mom only needed two seconds in her room, the scene of the crime, before her face went red with anger. She'd never heard her mom really yell before, but she yelled that day. Her dad was worse. He looked so sad and disappointed with Lindsay that he couldn't even talk to her. They grounded her for two weeks and took her television and her computer away. Her dad read her all kinds of really horrible stories about what smoking did to the body that he'd printed from the internet.

Long before she ever watched a single episode of *CSI*, Lindsay learned all about evidence. Just because she was not caught in the act didn't mean she had gotten away with anything. Not only had her room stunk of the smoke, but Kate had left the used match on the window frame.

What happened to her that night was similar.

After dinner, around sunset, Lindsay walked out onto the porch, and looked out at the ocean. She felt miserable about Mark. It was like he was already gone. Like she already missed him. A sound on the side of the house, Mark's side, drew her attention, and she crossed to the railing and looked down the alley.

Jack stood in the sand just outside Mark's window. His hands were on his hips as he looked down at the ground. Fear shot through Lindsay in fast, cold bolts.

She spun away, her mind racing as she replayed the afternoon in her head. What had she dropped? What evidence had she left behind? The realization came on soon after she exhausted her memories of the day.

The sand. She had left footprints in the sand.

Damn.

Soon she heard voices. Doug must have joined his partner outside Mark's window. They spoke rapidly, quietly. The voices were like a breeze ruffling papers, and though she struggled to hear the conversation, she could not make out the words.

With her heart slamming her ribs, sending a deafening pulse to her ears, she began to fear for Mark. If things were so bad before, what horrible punishment would they come up with now?

Finally words drifted out of the yard between the houses, words she could hear and understand. The cold bolts of fear shot even faster.

"We have to talk to her parents," one of the guardians said. "If that doesn't work, we'll have to get serious."

"I just want to kill the bastard."

"If only we could" was the reply.

They're capable of things you can't even imagine.

Lindsay walked south on the beach. To her right were houses, all lit up for evening; to her left the ocean, deep and black, spread out and joined the sky. Mostly, Lindsay looked at the sand. All of the ridges and dents from a day's use lay accusingly at her feet.

How could I have been so stupid?

She shook her head, gave the sand a good kick, and kept walking. She wanted distance between herself and her uncle's house. Even now, one or both of Mark's guardians might be talking to her parents, lying to them about Mark so they could keep him prisoner and keep her away. Or they might be punishing him. She didn't know; she just knew she needed to be somewhere else for a while.

145

She'd thought about sticking around and confronting the men. Ultimately, she couldn't. What if she said something that revealed the extent of her knowledge? In her eagerness to defend Mark, she could make matters worse. No. She needed to think this out, come up with a plan. Her heart ached over what those two might do to Mark, but if she was going to help him—really help him— she had to play it cool.

When she looked up from the sand, Lindsay saw that she was on the outskirts of the trailer village. People stood around their mobile homes, chatting and barbecuing. Closer to the water, two boys played catch with a football, the many lights from the trailers providing just enough glow to see the ball.

Beyond the trailers were more homes like her uncle's. Then the beaches gave way to rocky ground before a mile of cliffside rose up. In the next cove a handful of glassy mansions had been built, but the hills above them were undeveloped. Scrub grasses and shrubs decorated that landscape. A forest ran to the south and inland just above the road that traced the edge of the cliffs high above the ocean. Her dad had taken her up there when she was a little girl. Like many things, it was beautiful from a distance, but kind of ugly up close.

One of the boys playing catch on the beach laughed loudly at something and Lindsay looked toward him. The boy farthest from her was face-down in the sand, kicking his legs like a baby having a tantrum. Then he sprang to his feet and did a silly little dance before spiking the ball in the sand.

She thought Mark deserved moments like this, moments of fun and freedom and silliness. Everyone deserved that.

Lindsay turned away from the playing boys. What she saw next made her skin go cold with fear.

She'd been followed. Jack stood just inside the light cast from the backside of the nearest trailer. His black shirt clung to a burly, muscled frame. Dark pools of shadow hid his eyes, but she knew he was looking at her.

Oh no, she thought. *Oh no. Oh no!*

She backed up and nearly fell on her butt when the sand gave under her step. Somehow she regained her balance and spun away, her throat and chest tight with fear. Lindsay took two steps forward, then stopped. The beach ahead was dark, except for the dull glow coming from the houses, leaving big gaps of blackness ahead. Would anyone be outside, witnesses that might keep the muscled Jack at a distance?

He could catch her anytime he wanted to, and home seemed very far away.

Lindsay twisted around to the mobile home park, her gaze landing first at the back of the trailer and the man standing there. Without the slightest hesitation, Jack stepped out of the shadows and crossed the sand to stand between Lindsay and the well-lit park.

Should she scream? If nothing else, it would bring people to her, exposing the man so he wouldn't dare do anything to her tonight. Panic clouded her thoughts and charged her system with frantic energy. She couldn't just stand there.

So Lindsay turned and ran. Several times she nearly lost her footing, almost crashing to the sand, but she righted herself and kept moving forward. She heard the guardian behind her, his feet shushing through the sand. But he wasn't running. Not yet anyway.

Was he just keeping an eye on her? Trying to scare her?

A sharp pain came up in her side. Running through sand was like running in glue, every step a burden. Her chest ached from drawing in harsh breaths. She hated being afraid. Hated Jack. He had no right to follow her. No right!

When she couldn't run anymore, Lindsay slowed down. Terrified and furious, she turned to confront the man chasing her.

But he wasn't there. Lindsay looked from the lighted homes to the black ocean, but the guardian was gone. At some point he gave up his pursuit, possibly realizing that he could do nothing to her.

Lindsay bent forward to rest her hands on her knees. She breathed hard, trying to rid her side of the stitch. Sweat dripped into her eyes, and she wiped it away with a trembling palm. Eventually, she caught her breath and the pain ceased. She straightened up, brushed her hair off of her face, and turned toward her uncle's house.

The man in the black T-shirt stood only three feet away from her!

✦ ✦ ✦

"We must talk," Jack said in a low, controlled voice. "You're in no danger from me."

The tone was meant to be soothing, but Lindsay was in no way put at ease. The man was frightening. After chasing her half a mile through the sand, he wasn't even winded. That wasn't normal. Nothing about this guy and his partner was normal.

"So you chased me down the beach?" she asked, angrily. "Yeah, that makes me feel warm and comfy."

"Sarcasm is a child's weapon," Jack said. "It won't help you here."

"What do you want?"

"A simple understanding," he said. "You've intruded on a very troubling situation. It will stop. You will forget about the things you've seen. You will forget about *him*. He is our burden, and in a few days' time, we will take him from here. Until then, you will keep well away from our charge. To do otherwise will result in unimaginable harm."

The threat creeped into her skin and bones, resting there like a layer of frost. This powerful man with the emotionless face and soothing voice was not simply trying to scare her away; he was dead serious. She didn't know what to say and was so frightened she couldn't have formed words if she wanted to. Instead, she searched the nighttime beach over his shoulders for any sign of rescue.

"He isn't what he appears," the man said. "Do you understand that?"

Though she did not understand it, Lindsay's paralysis broke enough for her to nod her head. She just wanted him to go away. She'd agree to anything if it would send him back to the dilapidated house.

"Have a meaningful life," Jack said.

Then he turned away. He walked several steps up the beach, then paused. After a moment, perhaps considering an additional threat, he continued into the darkness.

Lindsay walked into her uncle's house through the back door and found her parents waiting for her in the living room. They sat together on the couch; her mom looked furious, and her dad looked sad, like someone just died.

Oh no, she thought. *The other one came here while his buddy followed me down the beach.*

She tried to ignore them, coolly walking to the

stairs as if nothing was wrong. But her mom stopped her.

"We need to have a word with you, young lady," she said.

Crap, Lindsay thought. *"Young lady" is not a good sign*.

She walked into the living room and met her mom's gaze, maintaining a cool expression. The last thing she wanted was a screaming match with her parents. It wouldn't do any good.

"What's up?" she asked.

"Mr. Richter from next door stopped by," her mom said. She paused, probably hoping her statement would send Lindsay into a fit of denial or argument. But Lindsay knew better than to react. Seeing that her daughter was not fazed, she continued. "He told us that you have been visiting with the boy who lives there."

"Um . . . and?" Lindsay said, surprised by how cool she sounded.

"He told us some really disturbing things," her dad said.

I'll bet, Lindsay thought, wondering what kinds of lies Doug Richter had told her parents. He'd probably made Mark out to be some kind of monster.

"Okay, but what does this have to do with me?" she asked.

"He's troubled," her mom said. "Mr. Richter told us that Mark has been in and out of institutions his whole life. The last time he was incarcerated was because he injured a little girl. She almost died, Lindsay."

That's exactly the kind of lie she would have expected, but it was crap, and she knew it. If Mark was that dangerous, they'd have bars on his windows, or they'd have him locked up. He wouldn't be separated from the world by a thin pane of glass. And she'd been in his room. Twice! They were totally alone, and he hadn't done a thing to harm her. Besides, there were laws. His guardians would have to tell neighbors if he was a threat, wouldn't they?

"Lindsay?" her dad asked.

"Yes?"

"Did you hear what your mom said?"

"I heard," she said. "But I don't see the issue."

"We're telling you to stay away from that boy."

"I know," she said. "I'm not arguing. I mean, I talked to him, but he was sort of creepy. He talked about some weird occult crap and wanted me to hang with him. Then he tried to hit on me and I was all, 'No chance in hell, Gomer.' I bailed. What's the crisis?"

The lie came so easily Lindsay wanted to keep telling it. A dozen little embellishments came to mind, but she stopped. If it was no big deal, as she'd said, she couldn't make it a big deal by talking about it too much.

"Oh," her mom said, suddenly deflated of her outrage. "We were given the impression that it was a bit more serious than that."

Lindsay laughed. "Whatever. I can understand them being cautious, but it's so not an issue."

"So we don't have to worry about you spending time over there?" her dad wanted to know.

"I wouldn't say that," Lindsay said. "I mean, have you seen the muscles on that other guy? He's full-on Hugh Jackman ripped. If *he* asked me out . . . well."

"Oh, stop it," her mom said. "Those men are old enough to be your father."

"Hot is hot," Lindsay said, putting on a mischievous grin.

"Go upstairs before you give me a stroke," her dad said.

Lindsay was checking email when her dad opened the door. "Okay if I come in?"

"Sure," she said, closing the laptop. She wasn't really concerned with him seeing anything. It was just a reflex.

Her dad walked across the room and sat on the bed next to her. "Is everyone back home surviving without you?"

"Barely," Lindsay said.

"I don't doubt it," he told her. Then her dad put a hand on her leg and patted it warmly. "I just want to make sure we're clear on a few things," he said.

"Okay."

"The man who came over today and the other one . . . Those men are social workers, and that boy is their ward. They are court-appointed guardians."

"I just thought they were his dads," Lindsay said, suddenly less comfortable with the lies. "I never thought to ask about it."

"Well, they aren't. His parents died a long time ago, and the kid's had a rough go of it, but that doesn't excuse what he's done. Or what he might do."

"No, it doesn't," Lindsay agreed. Of course, she knew he hadn't done anything.

"Good," her dad said, rising from the bed. "I'm glad you see it that way. I mean I know you didn't want to be here. We kind of dragged you away from your life, and I figure you're still upset about that."

"I'm not upset."

"You were. And you had a right to be. I was being selfish. I knew you didn't want to spend time with us. You're growing up and have friends and plans, and next year you'll have more friends and more plans. The year after that, you'll be a senior and then you'll go to college. I figured this was the last time we'd be spending any real time together, and I wanted that."

Lindsay said nothing.

"I know I'm going to miss spending time with you," her dad continued. "Hell, I already do. You're my favorite person in the world."

Before Lindsay could say anything else, her dad left the room and closed the door.

She hadn't been this close to tears in a very long time.

When morning came, the sky was overcast with a summer storm. Lindsay snuggled into the comforter and looked at the window, resisting the urge to run to it and look out. Instead she climbed out of bed and went downstairs. As always, her parents met her in the kitchen. They seemed happy and relaxed, the issue of the boy next door resolved in their minds.

"No beach today," her dad announced. "It's supposed to rain."

"That blows," Lindsay said. But she didn't really mind. Actually, she'd been thinking of doing something else all night. "Maybe we could hit the outlet mall? It didn't look too far from town."

Both her parents perked up at the suggestion: her mom because it meant shopping, one of the few passions they shared; her dad because it meant the whole family would be spending time together the way he wanted. Lindsay didn't have to say another word about it.

In her room, she took her laptop off the window seat. She couldn't help but look outside, but she never got the chance to peer into Mark's window. The man that called himself Mr. Richter, the man Mark called Doug, stood on the sand below. His head cocked upward to stare at Lindsay's window.

You ass, Lindsay thought, quickly backing away from the glass. She carried her laptop to the bed and powered it up. Lindsay spent thirty minutes reading and answering emails. She promised to call Kate when she got back from shopping with her parents. Then she logged off and went across the hall to shower.

She had a busy day ahead.

By the time her dad pulled the SUV into the massive parking lot of the Rocky Shores Mall, the rain was coming down hard. Though the storm didn't even compare to the one that marked their first day of vacation, the downpour was substantial. Apparently the mall was a favored place for locals during foul weather, because the parking lot was almost full when they arrived.

Finally her dad found a space on the far end of the lot. They only had a single umbrella, so huddled together, they dashed for the covered walkway that ran in and around the outlet stores. Her dad laughed as he trotted along holding the umbrella over their heads. Her mom complained good-naturedly.

At first Lindsay stayed close to her parents. Her dad was having such a good time he bought her three blouses at Banana Republic and insisted she try more on. It was kind of like Christmas, only Lindsay got to pick out all of her own gifts. At the Coach store, her dad bought himself a new wallet and a belt. Her mom even considered a new purse, but ultimately talked herself out of the purchase.

After a couple of hours, Lindsay hoisted her bags and went off on her own. Her dad wanted to explore the Ralph Lauren store, and her mom needed to visit the Mikasa outlet. Lindsay took the opportunity and told her parents she would be at the Gap, looking at shorts. It wasn't a lie.

She did go to the Gap to buy shorts, but they weren't for her. She'd hugged Mark, and he was about the same size as her first boyfriend, Todd. As a result, she had a good idea about his waist size. She chose two pairs—oatmeal and khaki. She stopped at a table loaded down with T-shirts and picked out three in a size that would actually fit him, unlike the black shirt he always wore. She made sure she picked bright, interesting colors. Mark was probably tired of black, probably hated the sight of it by now.

She couldn't believe his guardians had taken all of his clothes. That was third-world cruelty. She'd never heard anything like it before.

She made a quick stop in the Nike store and bought an inexpensive blue gym bag. She finished her shopping in just less than thirty minutes, which still gave her plenty of time before she was to meet her parents in the food court for a late lunch. Walking by the GNC, she noticed a display for protein bars and decided she would buy some of those for Mark.

If he were really running away, he'd need them.

Lindsay returned to the food court and nearly

stumbled to a stop in the doorway. Tee and Mel sat at a table halfway across the room. So much had happened in the last few days, Lindsay had all but forgotten the girls, but there they were, flipping their platinum hair and talking a mile a minute over sodas, totally engrossed in each other's words. That ended soon enough, though. As if a bell sounded over the food court door, both girls turned their heads and saw her.

Tee and Mel lowered their chins and looked at her harshly. Lindsay felt like turning and running, but instead, she stood her ground. She didn't know what Ev had said about her, trying to cover her ass for scamming on Mark, but it was probably nasty. No doubt Tee and Mel were full-on against her now because Ev told them to be. If they knew Ev's plan to ditch them, they might not be so loyal.

Lindsay strolled into the court and walked across to the Electra-Juice. She ordered herself a strawberry smoothie and waited while the pimple-faced boy made it for her. She could almost feel the girls at her back, even before one of them spoke.

"Hey," Mel said.

Lindsay turned slowly, noticed the girls, and

then turned back to the counter. Whatever. She had nothing to say to the bonfire club.

"We're talking to you," Tee announced, grabbing Lindsay's arm.

She spun around, shaking off Tee's grip.

"What is with you?" Tee asked. "We're all cool to you. We let you in, let you be one of us, and you spit all over it? Who do you think you are?"

"Yeah," Mel said.

"I didn't ask to be in," Lindsay snapped. "You and Ev can bite my ass."

"Ev was nothing but cool to you."

"She tried to snare my boyfriend," Lindsay said. It was close enough to the truth.

"Oh, right," Mel scoffed. "Like Ev would *have* to *try*?"

"You would so lose," Tee added. "Whatever. Look, we were just coming over to tell you Ev was sick and all. We didn't see you at the hospital and you never called us back. We thought you might care, but obviously you don't give a crap."

Ev was in the hospital? The news came as a shock. No wonder Mel and Tee gave her such nasty looks. They thought Lindsay was still Ev's friend, and she hadn't even visited her. That also explained why Char wasn't with them. If Ev was sick, Char would never leave her bedside.

"I didn't know she was sick," Lindsay said, feeling awful. "I'm sorry."

"Yeah. Sure you are." Tee crossed her arms over her chest.

"Is she okay?"

"Like *you* care," Mel said. "She's having this total nervous breakdown, and you stand here talking trash about her. I do *not* think so."

"Oh my god," Lindsay whispered, shocked. "I didn't know."

"Whatevs!" Tee said. She spun on her heels.

Mel did the same, and a moment later they both walked away through the crowded food court.

In her room at her uncle's house, Lindsay removed tags from the shorts she'd bought Mark. She folded the shorts and the T-shirts. She placed everything in the blue gym bag. As she did so, she thought about Mel and Tee. Thought about Ev.

A nervous breakdown? That was awful.

What did she see in Mark's room?

Lindsay tried to fold that thought and put it away, like another pair of shorts. More than likely

Ev was on her way to crazy before that night. She was so young and suddenly faced with all of this pressure in her career, and she snapped. That was logical enough. Lindsay wanted to believe it, but didn't. Something had driven Ev out of her mind.

She saw Mark's guardians in that room.

They perform these rituals sometimes.

Ev stumbled onto one of these rituals, and it must have been horrible.

Like I said, some of that junk is just full-on creepy.

But why were they performing rituals in Mark's room? God, what were they going to do to him? Lindsay went to the window and looked out. The shade was down over Mark's window. He couldn't even call her. He couldn't call for help because he'd returned her cell phone. He was alone down there, trapped in that house with two men who were becoming more and more dangerous.

Lindsay zipped up the blue gym bag, now filled with supplies for Mark. Would she get the chance to give it to him?

"Are you like totally in love with him?" Kate gushed.

"No," Lindsay said. "God, I hardly know him."

"Has he kissed you yet?"

"Yes."

"You totally have to stick to our pact. Even if you are on vacation. It still counts."

"Don't be a freak, Kate."

Lindsay hadn't even thought about the pact in months. Last year, after watching *Titanic* for the billionth time, they swore to each other that they wouldn't go all the way until they were really, totally, completely in love. It had to be a Leo-Kate kind of love or else it didn't count. Looking back on it now, Lindsay found the pact rather childish and wondered why she ever agreed to it in the first place. It was like two little girls swearing they would only marry princes or something.

"So, is he taking you out or what?"

"Not really," Lindsay said. "There's no place to go but the beach. So we just kind of hang around the house."

That wasn't too much of a lie.

"I'm so jealous," Kate said. "I can't believe you snared yourself a boyfriend. No one's ever going to talk to me again, not after the tragic fun-suck of a party."

"Trey said he had a great time," Lindsay assured

for the fourth time. "He said everyone had a really good time. Well, except for Constance."

"She's such a skank engine. She knew I liked Chad. I totally told her last week, and the first thing she does is climb on him. At my party! In my BED!"

Then Kate launched into another ten-minute rant about the girls at school and how she didn't trust any of them, except for Lindsay of course. Lindsay grunted and said, "yeah," in all the right places. She knew how girls could be. She'd seen Ev in action.

Instead of feeling angry when she thought about Ev, Lindsay found herself feeling sorry for the girl. It was strange. She didn't like Ev, but she pitied her. Ev was calculating and driven and would have done anything to escape Redlands Beach. It was her one dream: to get out. But she wouldn't get out now. She'd seen something that drove her crazy, and traded the glamour of a blossoming career for a hospital bed in a psychiatric ward.

"Are you seeing him tomorrow?" Kate asked.

"What?" Lindsay said. "Oh. Depends on his dads."

She crossed to the window again and looked out. Mr. Richter stood beneath the scraggly tree, facing the house.

"They're really strict," Lindsay said.

"That's weird. Rachel's moms are totally cool. Maybe it's a guy thing."

"Yeah," Lindsay said, forcing a laugh. "It might be."

She wanted to spill everything to Kate, wanted to tell her about Mark's abusive guardians. How he was all alone with them. How he couldn't contact help. She wanted to tell her best friend about Ev, and how she'd melted down after seeing something in that house. She wanted to let Kate know that she was going to help Mark. It wasn't much, just a few supplies to get him started.

She didn't take the chance telling Kate, though. She couldn't. Not yet. When it was all done and Mark was safely away, Lindsay would tell Kate everything. Until then, she needed to stay quiet.

The rain finally stopped. Her parents announced they were going to take "a snooze for about an hour." Lindsay returned to her room and went to the window.

She was surprised to note that neither Doug nor Jack stood in the yard, at least no place where she could see them. She was more surprised to see Mark in his window, looking up at her. He waved his arm frantically for her to come over. He looked totally desperate to talk to her.

Lindsay rushed down the stairs and out the door. At the side of the house, she paused, wondering how she would get near his window without leaving tracks in the sand. The answer appeared quickly enough.

Like her uncle's house, Mark's sat up off the ground, giving way to low thatches of grass. All Lindsay had to do was cling to the side of the house and step on those. Sure she would still leave prints, but they wouldn't be nearly as obvious as tromping through the sand. She moved fast but carefully from one tuft of grass to the next.

At Mark's window, she peered in. He stood on the other side of the small desk, looking absolutely miserable. His eyes were swollen as if he'd been crying. Dark circles painted the puffy skin beneath. He looked very thin and quite ill.

Lindsay put her palms against the glass and pulled, but it didn't budge. Inside, Mark shook his head.

"They locked it," he called.

"Are you okay?" Lindsay asked, trying to make her voice just loud enough for Mark to hear, but not so loud it carried to her parents' room at the front of her uncle's house.

He shook his head. Moving slowly as if in great pain, Mark grabbed the hem of his T-shirt and pulled it over his head. Lindsay looked through the dirty glass, remembering her first view of him, topless and smoothly muscular. Her eyes roamed over his perfect pale skin, his wonderful abs, and she squinted, wondering what it was Mark wanted her to see.

Head low, like a beaten dog, Mark turned around.

Lindsay saw his back and gasped. Her stomach clenched tight and her throat closed with horror. She put a hand over her mouth to keep from screaming.

Two dark circles about the size of bracelets were carved or burned into Mark's back. The filthy glass and gloomy bedroom made it hard to tell exactly how the wounds were inflicted. But there they were, two circles filled with complex swirls and lines, etched on Mark's skin. They were puffy and red and recently scabbed over. They were awful.

"My god," Lindsay whimpered, already crying from the horrible sight.

Mark turned back to her. He didn't bother putting his shirt on.

"I think they're going to kill me," he said, his

voice barely loud enough for Lindsay to hear. "I tried to leave and they did this. They're going to kill me."

"No, they won't," Lindsay said, sniffing and wiping the tears from her eyes. "I won't let them."

"You can't do anything," Mark said. "I told you before."

"It's going to be okay," Lindsay said. "Just hold on. Okay? I'll be right back."

Again Mark nodded his head.

Lindsay needed to get the gym bag and then get Mark out of that house, but it was so damn hard to leave him. He needed her and shouldn't be alone. She wiped the freshest of her tears away, then eased along the side of the house.

She looked back one last time, seeing only the angle of the window. Then she stepped onto the sand and headed for the porch of her uncle's house. Inside, she hurried quietly up the stairs. In her room she grabbed the blue gym bag and her tote, which carried her cell phone, Treo, and wallet.

Back in the hall, she was heading for the stairs when the door to her parents' room opened. Lindsay froze.

"Everything okay?" her dad whispered.

"Sure," Lindsay said, hearing the tremble in her own voice. *Be cool,* she thought. *Be cool.* "I was just running down to the boardwalk for a bit."

"Is it still raining?" her dad wanted to know.

"No. It stopped."

"Good," he said quietly. "I was hoping we'd get some more sun. I wanted to grill out tonight. Have a good time. Be careful."

"I will," she said, looking at her father's kind round face. He looked sleepy, but also concerned. Maybe he didn't believe her. She forced a smile and waved quickly.

She'd get Mark out of the house and then come home. Her parents wouldn't even know. It would be over in a few minutes.

Outside, she dashed across the sand to Mark, the blue bag and her tote striking her hips in turn. No longer worried about leaving prints in the sand, she raced through the alley right up to the window. Mark stood inside, looking dazed.

"You have to go," Lindsay said. "Come on."

Mark blinked and then his eyes grew wide when he began to understand what she was saying.

"I can't," Mark said. "I can't open the window.

You'll have to break it."

What? Why couldn't he open the window? Lindsay didn't understand, but she had no time to question him. She looked around the sand until she found a good-sized rock. Gripping it tightly, she smashed the glass near the lock, reached in, and unlatched the frame. She slid open the window and waited for Mark to climb out.

But he didn't move.

"Get out of there!" Lindsay said, her voice trembling with desperation.

"Give me the rock," Mark whispered.

"What are you talking about?"

"Just give it to me."

Lindsay did as he asked, anxious for him to get moving. With a high toss, the stone flew through the window and into Mark's hand.

Behind him, the door slammed open. Jack stood on the threshold. Before the door even crashed against the wall, he was already shouting gibberish at Mark, waving his hands in the air like a stage magician trying to sell a trick.

A tiny smile pushed up the corners of Mark's mouth. He spun and hurled the rock at Jack. It connected solidly with the burly man's forehead.

Jack's eyes rolled up. He staggered, then fell over the threshold into Mark's room, hitting the floor facedown.

"Bastard," Mark spat.

He stepped forward and reached out a hand toward the opening to the hall. He snatched his fingers back when they reached the threshold. He tried again. Mark shoved his hand into the doorway as if testing the air, wiggled his fingers.

"Thanks, pal," he said to the unconscious form of Jack. Then he stepped out of the room.

Lindsay jogged along the house to meet Mark at the porch. When she rounded the corner, Mark was already standing on the sand in front of her. Startled by his speed, Lindsay jumped a bit. Then Mark's arms went around her in a tight hug that nearly cut off her breath.

"I can't believe you did this for me," he said. "Thank you. Thank you."

Lindsay's legs grew weak, and she fell against Mark, letting his strength hold her up. He felt so good next to her; he felt absolutely perfect. She didn't want the embrace to end, but it had to end. He needed to get away from this house and this beach, and he needed to do it fast.

"You have to go," she whispered, feeling so sad she could barely finish the sentence.

"I don't think I'll make it very far," Mark said, sounding terribly weak.

"You have to try."

"They hurt me pretty bad," he said. "My back."

"We have to get you someplace safe," Lindsay told him.

"You'll go with me?" he asked.

"I'll get you someplace safe," she said, burying her face in his neck, holding him as tightly as her arms would allow.

The sand squished under her feet as she helped Mark across the beach. At first Lindsay suggested they walk along the road so he could hitchhike, but Mark thought they might be spotted, perhaps by his guardians. Lindsay knew he was right.

When they reached the trailer park, Lindsay saw a festive afternoon was in full swing. Adults barbecued, drank beer, talked, and laughed. Kids played on the sand near the water, throwing foot- balls and playing tag with the waves, chasing them out and dashing away when the surf came in.

Mark stopped and tightened his grip around Lindsay's shoulder. He leaned down and quietly spoke in her ear.

"I can't believe you got me out. I can't believe it. It feels and smells and tastes so good out here. I want to do and see everything all over again."

They made their way through the encampment. Mark tried to smile and wave at the happy people enjoying their time on the beach. But he was leaning on her heavily for support. He was trying to make it look like they were a young couple in love. Lindsay tried to do the same, but with all of these strange eyes on her, she was worried. She kept her head down and to the side, as if in shame, nestling her cheek against Mark's chest as she guided him to the other side of the trailer park.

At the point where the beach turned rocky, Mark paused. He turned to Lindsay and kissed her.

His soft lips pushed against hers, sending electric tingles through her body. *This is* the *kiss,* Lindsay thought. All of the other kisses in her life were bland and meaningless compared to this.

They held each other tightly, mouths joined, bodies fitting together perfectly like two puzzle pieces. Lindsay's head was light with passion. She felt like she was floating, or rather flying, and Mark was the one making it happen. In his arms she felt safe and alive and happy. So happy.

Mark pulled away from her, smiling. "I'm starving," he said. "Those guys haven't fed me in like two days."

Lindsay put the blue gym bag on the sand and unzipped the side compartment. She dug inside and retrieved an energy bar. Proudly she presented it to him.

Mark snatched it from her hand and tore into it. Once his mouth was filled with half an energy bar, his eagerness dimmed. He looked embarrassed. "Sorry," he said. "I'm just really hungry."

"Are they okay?" Lindsay asked. "I didn't really know what to get."

"They're great," Mark said. He swallowed hard. "What I really want is a steak. A big bloody steak with about three pounds of French fries. But I guess I won't be having steak for a while. This is good, though. Thanks."

He pulled her close for another kiss. She wrapped her arms around him, careful not to rub too hard on his back. She knew the circular wounds there would have to be treated. But she needed to get him safe first. Find someplace where he could hide for the night.

"Where should we go?" she asked once the

embrace ended. "I can't just leave you on the beach."

"There's a house on the other side of these rocks. It's in a private cove. It's been empty for weeks."

"How do you know that?" Lindsay asked.

"Oh," Mark said, his eyes twinkling, "you'd be surprised what I know."

They stood inside, looking through a window.

Surrounded by high walls of black rock and facing the ocean across a vast, fan-shaped beach, the house was amazing. It was huge and modern, totally gorgeous and completely empty. On the beach side of the house, glass ran from the immaculate marble-tiled floors to the ceiling twenty-five feet above, giving a breathtaking view of the cove, the seething ocean, and the sky. Lindsay and Mark stood before this panorama, arms wrapped around each other's waists. Lindsay was in awe. She couldn't even imagine how wonderful the house must have been with furniture, lights, and well-dressed people walking over the floors, which were now frosted with a layer of dust.

"It's just so beautiful," Lindsay said. "But how

could you have known? You've been locked in that house for so long."

"I heard Jack and Doug talking about it. It was way too expensive for them, but they gave it some serious thought."

"I can see why."

"I used to live in a house like this," he said. "Way up north in New York. The Hamptons. It seems like a hundred years ago. Everyone was just happy and cruel and oblivious."

"Happy and cruel?" Lindsay asked.

"Happy to own anything they wanted. Happy to do whatever they wanted. Completely cruel to those who had nothing."

"It sounds terrible."

"Only if you had nothing. It was actually okay. You get a real sense of human nature when you hang out with people who never have to deal with the consequences of their actions. I knew one guy who strangled his wife, dumped her in the bathtub, and acted like nothing happened. The police knew he killed her. They knew damn well she didn't drown in the tub, but since this guy had more money than God, no one lifted a finger."

"It's just not fair."

"I could tell you a thousand stories like that. People aren't really that good at heart, but they are afraid. That's what keeps most of them in line."

Lindsay didn't know what to say to that. She believed people tried to be good, and didn't think it necessarily came down to fear. No normal person actually wanted to hurt, *really hurt*, another person.

"What are we going to do?" she asked. "I mean, I can't stay. Will you be all right?"

"I'll be okay," Mark said, putting his hand on the window. "But damn, I want to be out there. I've spent so much time looking at the world through glass that standing here, even with you, is making me crazy. I know we have to be careful, but I just want to run around in the sand under the moon and smell the ocean. Man, I can't wait to be a thousand miles away from here so I can just be outside!"

"Once you're better," Lindsay said, "you can go anyplace you want."

"But I won't have you," Mark said, sounding sad and lost.

He kissed her again, a long and slow kiss. His tongue moved in slow rhythms against hers, making her heart tremble with excitement.

"It's all because of you," he said, pulling away. "You're my salvation."

Then they were kissing again. Mark ran his hands up her body, rested them on her breasts as he unfastened the first button of her blouse. A bolt of fear raced through Lindsay.

Was this really happening? Did she want this to happen?

Head swimming with crazy thoughts, her body alight with passion, Lindsay decided the answer to both questions was yes.

She woke up from a deep sleep, cold and aching. It was dark. Night had fallen. She reached out for Mark, but her hand found nothing but cool marble. Lindsay rolled onto her back and let out a small groan of pain. Her entire body felt bruised and stiff. Brushing a lock of hair from her face, she stared at the dark ceiling, unsure of the emotions colliding in her head.

She'd done it. They'd done it. They made love. It was hard to believe. It seemed like a strange, fluid dream to her. While it was happening, she wasn't even thinking about the act, merely experiencing it. Oh, it was wonderful, but also frightening and painful and confusing. With so many conflicting thoughts, not once did she think about the fact that they hadn't used protection. She was so caught up in the moment, the sensations.

It'll be okay, she told herself. *We only did it once. Next time we'll be careful.* But as she thought this, she felt a strange movement low in her body, a twitch, as if something already lived inside her. The feeling paralyzed her with panic. She breathed hard, in and out, telling herself it was just her imagination, her childish fear. *It'll be okay,* she repeated to herself when the dread got too bad to manage.

Once the panic passed and she could again think clearly, Lindsay sat up on the floor and blinked. Mark stood at the window, the big glowing moon hovering just above his shoulder. He wore a pair of the shorts she bought him at the outlet mall. They fit perfectly, as she'd known they would. The muscles in his back flexed as he leaned forward on the window, pressing his forehead on the glass. The round wounds looked like black holes in his skin. Was he crying, or just relieved to be free at last?

"Mark?" she asked.

Something moved under the skin of his back.

Low ridges bulged and writhed, distorting his badly scarred skin as if plump eels slid just beneath the surface of him.

"You don't know me," he said to the glass.

"I love you," Lindsay said, growing more frightened by the moment.

"Do you?" he asked, his voice low and hollow as if he spoke into a vast cave.

Mark turned—but it wasn't Mark anymore.

"This is what Ev saw," he growled. "Do you love this?"

The face was distorted, as if covered in melted wax. It was thick with ridges and lumps. The eel-like movement beneath his skin grew frantic. His pectorals swelled to an impossible size while his waist shrank in so tightly that the shorts fell from his hips. The creature that was Mark stepped out of the shorts. He raced toward Lindsay, his entire body blurred by his speed.

Lindsay screamed as the terrible creature descended on her, clawed hands reaching for her face.

Then she woke for real.

Lindsay sat up on the marble, her scream still echoing in the vast, empty room. She clutched her blouse together in front and quickly buttoned it against the cold. The windows before her showed the shimmering blanket of night sea and night sky. The fat moon of her dream was still there, hovering high above the water.

But where was Mark?

"Mark?"

She climbed into her shorts and spoke his name again. Icy marble met the soles of her feet, sending chills up her legs. Why was it so cold? They wouldn't just leave the air conditioner running—not for an empty house. Lindsay hugged herself tightly and wandered through the living room to the dining area. Here, too, she found a wall of glass with a spectacular view of the cove, but instead of finding the panorama beautiful, it frightened her, made her feel removed from the familiar and alone.

"Mark?" she called.

A noise rose behind her, merely a whisper like papers blowing down a sidewalk. She turned quickly, but not fast enough.

Jack's square face, a red welt at the center of his forehead, rushed through the darkness, his hands already raised to grab her.

Lindsay screamed. She fought, slapping her fists down on Jack's muscular shoulders as his hands locked around her biceps. She kicked at his crotch, but he lifted a knee, turned slightly and blocked the kick. Her shin collided with his and pain exploded along the bone.

"You can't do this," she cried.

"Quiet!" Jack snapped. With a blurring motion, he spun Lindsay and locked an arm around her throat. He covered her mouth with a palm and pulled her tight to his chest. "You foolish child," he whispered in her ear. "Do you have any idea what you've done? What you've *unleashed*?"

Lindsay couldn't breathe. Jack's grip did not cover her nose, but she was too frightened to draw breath. It felt like her entire body was made of stone like the floor beneath her feet, except for her heart, which pounded frantically as if trapped inside her body and trying to escape.

Jack walked her forward, back to the living room. She saw Mark standing in the middle of the room. Her captor paused on the threshold, his muscles growing more rigid against her.

Thank god, she thought. Mark would save her.

She looked at him hopefully, eyes wide. Dull moon-light painted the left side of his face.

"Jesus," Jack whispered.

"'Fraid not," Mark said with a smile. "Don't think even he could save you now."

"You have no magic," Jack said. "You wear the binding signs. I know. I burned them into your back."

"Yeah, about that," Mark said, reaching for the hem of his shirt and pulling it over his head. "I gotta admit that hurt." He tossed his shirt on the floor and threw his arms out like he was surrendering. "But it didn't hurt nearly as much as this did."

He turned, slowly revealing his back.

Lindsay gagged, then felt her throat clamp shut.

The skin on Mark's back was gone—torn away in long strips, leaving the glistening bulges of his muscles. Blood ran over the waist and butt of his shorts. Bits of flesh hung like thick threads at his sides. Lindsay couldn't bear to see it, so she looked away into the corner, and there she saw the shredded strips of skin, which were piled up like a bloody old shirt. She swallowed hard and looked back at the boy.

Mark completed his turn, the smile still on his

face. "I'm going to take my time with you, Little Jacky. I've got a lot of payback due me." Mark stepped forward, his chest expanding with a deep breath. "Do you remember what I did to that girl in Denver? Oh, she had it easy compared to what you've got coming."

"Stay back," Jack said, his voice like a loud-speaker in Lindsay's ear. "Paralyze," he muttered. "Freeze muscle and bone and blood and breath."

"Knock it off, Jacky," Mark said, taking another casual step forward. "You don't have any of your pills and potions now. Word magic isn't going to do a damn thing against me, and you know it."

Lindsay didn't understand what she was seeing. Mark's back was gone. How could he even stand up?

She mumbled his name against the thick palm covering her mouth.

"Oh," Mark said, fixing his clear blue eyes on hers, "you still don't get it, do you? I'm the monster of this story, little girl. Lester Krohl knew it. Barbie sure as hell knew it. I'm the Big Bad Wolf, the Boogeyman, and the Wicked Witch all rolled up into one."

No, Lindsay thought, her eyes filling with tears. *No, it isn't true*.

"Tell her, Little Jacky," Mark said, seeming to take absolute glee in the moment. "Tell her how very bad *I* am."

"He's one of Lucifer's spawn," Jack whispered. "He is evil and darkness manifest unto man. He is a moral disease."

"And you and your buddies tried to break my groove," Mark said, now only five steps away. "How long's it been? Ten years? Twenty?"

"You have been under the brotherhood's guard for thirty-two years."

"Well, time flies," Mark said.

Jack pulled Lindsay back a step and then another. Her head was growing light. She tried to keep from fainting, but already, the room behind Mark's back spun and blurred, though he remained in focus, unchanged.

"Now, where's that buddy of yours?" Mark asked. "We can't have a party without him."

"I'm here, boy," Doug Richter said from the open doorway at Mark's back. He held a shotgun against his shoulder and sighted down the barrel.

"Well, what have you got there?" Mark asked. "A pop gun?"

"Yes," Doug said. He pulled the trigger, and Mark

was lifted from the floor. He crashed into the wall with a sickening *thunk* and slid to the floor.

Lindsay screamed against the palm, only to find it hastily removed. Jack's arm left her throat and his hands were clutching her shoulders, pushing her forward.

"We don't have much time," Jack said, ushering her away from Mark's body toward Doug. "Come on. You can't be here."

Doug lowered the shotgun and threw out an arm, blocking Lindsay and Jack. "She can't leave. Not yet," he said.

"She isn't safe here," Jack said.

"What's happening?" Lindsay cried.

"We have to finish this," Doug continued. "He has to be bound. We can't just leave him, and I can't do this alone."

Lindsay looked from Jack to Doug. The two older men now appeared heroic to her, not frightening.

"Yes," he said. Sweat covered Jack's face, and his burly torso trembled. "Yes. But we have to protect her."

"The icons," Doug said. "Do you have them?"

Jack nodded. He drove a hand deep into his

pockets and pulled out half a dozen of the strange corner pieces Lindsay first saw framing Mark's window. She remembered their placement. Mark had said they were meant to keep evil out, but he lied. They were meant to keep evil in, meant to keep Mark trapped in his room. She understood that now. But what difference did it make? Mark was dead. Doug shot him.

"Put her in the coat closet," Doug said, jabbing his finger at a door on the far side of the foyer. "They won't protect her from all sides, but it's all we can do now."

Jack latched on to Lindsay's biceps again and dragged her painfully across the foyer to a simple-looking door.

"I want to go home," Lindsay cried. She wanted to see her parents, wanted to hold them and know they were okay. "Can't I just go home?"

"There isn't time," Jack said. He pulled open the closet door and flung Lindsay inside. She hit the back wall hard, and her legs nearly went out from under her. "If we don't stop him, he'll come for you, because you know what he is. He won't let you or your family live, and he will make you suffer."

Jack flipped one of the icons into the air and caught it with his right hand. With a powerful thrust, he drove the metal spike into the corner of the doorframe. With a violent twist, he screwed it into position. Another icon flew into the air, and this one also found itself buried in the wood. He knelt down, intending to affix additional metal pieces to the lower corners of the door, but paused.

The floor was marble.

Lindsay watched with mounting panic. She didn't want to be a captive of the two old men. She lunged forward, but Jack threw a palm toward her, struck her chest, and sent her back against the wall.

"I'm trying to protect you," he growled.

"Let me go!" she screamed. She didn't know what they were trying to do, but she didn't feel safe, and she wanted to *leave*! Again she charged for the opening.

Jack sprang to his feet, and she hit his chest. It felt harder than the wall at her back. She shrank away. The man returned to his knees.

Seeing no other choice, he drove one of the icons through the grout separating the wooden frame from the marble. He twisted it deep, but it stuck out at an odd angle, not nearly as even as the ones higher up. Jack repeated the action with the last icon.

"Those won't keep me in here," Lindsay said.

"They aren't meant to keep you in," Jack said, standing up and rolling his shoulders as if trying to break tension out of them. "They're meant to keep him out."

"He's dead," Lindsay said.

"No," Jack told her. "He isn't. He can't be killed, not by metal or magic or any other weapon of man. He can only be contained. His influence is eternal, from the beginning of time until the sun burns dark." He looked away toward Doug, who stood over Mark's body.

The tall man held a round piece of metal like a massive coin in his hand, and bounced it on his palm.

Jack turned back to Lindsay, his face set in an expression of deepest sorrow. "I'm very sorry," he said. "You're going to see some terrible things."

Lindsay watched Jack step away from the closet. He closed the front door and threw the locks, fixing the chain with a decisive *clack*. Then he stomped across the room, waving his hand at Doug Richter.

"Give me the brand," Jack said. "And shoot him again. He's playing possum."

"Now why would you go and tattle like that?" Mark asked from his place on the floor.

Startled, Lindsay leaped. Mark couldn't be alive. The shotgun blast had hit him in the middle of the back—*a back flayed of its skin, ripped away by Mark's own hands.*

She shivered and retreated to the wall. She could

195

still see the whole room. She saw Jack catch the metallic talisman in his hand, saw Doug snatching at the floor for his shotgun. And she saw Mark. Mark who should be dead. Mark who wasn't human.

He rolled over, pressed himself against the wall, and in a flash was on his feet. A moment later, moving too quickly for Lindsay to track, he stood in front of the window. The smile was gone from Mark's face. Fury bent his mouth and weighed his brow.

"Welcome to the pain," he said.

Suddenly the air was alive with movement. Lindsay squinted, trying to understand exactly what she was seeing, but it made no sense. It looked like the film of dust that covered the floor was rising like smoke to fill the room. The thin gray clouds began to tighten and grow dense, forming dozens of long, twisting ropes. As Doug Richter lifted the shotgun to his shoulder, one of the strands of dust whipped out and lashed his face and forearm.

He cried out and dropped the gun just as a second coil struck his neck with a fierce snapping sound. Jack ran across the room, holding the disk he'd called the brand in front of him. A strip of flesh from the gory mound in the corner snaked out and coiled around his ankle, sending him crashing to the hard stone floor. He rolled over, tried to get to his feet, but three more strips of bloody skin shot forward, wrapped around his ankles and wrists, pulled him into a spread eagle, and dragged him high into the air. The brand fell from his hand and clacked on the marble floor.

Doug struggled with the coil at his throat, digging his fingers into his own skin to get under the constricting noose. A rope of twisting dust formed above his head like a slender tornado and dipped down to join the end of the noose. Once the two coils touched, they fused together, and Doug was jerked toward the ceiling.

Both men hung in the air like marionettes. Their bodies dipped and swung as they struggled, but they could not break free of Mark's bonds.

"Stop it!" Lindsay screamed from her place in the closet. "Mark, you have to stop this."

He swung his head toward her furiously, like a starving wolf catching her scent. "You think you can tell *me* what to do? You think you command *me*? I've owned you and controlled you since the moment I saw you."

"No," Lindsay said, but her throat was as dry as the dust.

"You were so easy to manipulate," Mark said. "So desperate to be necessary."

Lindsay's fear and misery hardened behind her ribs, turned to anger. She stepped forward, but Jack shouted, "Don't."

Mark looked into the air at Jack's bound form.

"He's trying to lure you out from behind the icons. He can't hurt you if you stay behind them."

"That's not true," Mark said. "Not true at all."

He stomped toward the closet, his blue eyes fixed on Lindsay. With a flourish he waved his left arm. Above him, the strips of skin holding Jack rippled. Then they whipped out, sending the burly man through the window. He screamed as the glass shattered into a thousand tiny pieces, and Jack disappeared into the darkness.

"Night Jack," Mark said, walking faster across the floor. "Night Dougy."

With another flourish, this time of his right arm, a dozen dirt devils spun across the room. When they reached Doug, they wrapped themselves around his kicking body like pythons. He dropped to the floor with a hard crack.

"Just the two of us," Mark said, reaching the closet door. He glared at her, his eyes like blue flames. "Just the way you wanted."

Lindsay hugged the back wall of the closet. "You son of a bitch."

"More accurate than you know," Mark said. "Now, about that pain?"

"Get away from me!" Lindsay cried.

"Or . . . ," he said, taking a step back. He threw his arms out, again in that pose of surrender. The tinkle of glass filled the room behind him. Something glimmered in the air over his shoulder, like a firefly. Then it seemed the air was full of fireflies, with lights flashing and fading. Only the swarm she witnessed was not living; it was made from the shards of glass. Like the dust, they defied gravity, moving like twinkling ghosts.

"Oh no," Lindsay whimpered.

"Those don't look terribly stable," Mark said, pointing at the low corners of the door. Lindsay looked down at the icons, their imperfect placement. "Little Jacky wasn't being very careful. I'll bet the glass will find a way in. All it takes is a tiny break in the veil, like when Jack fell over the threshold of my room. Such a minor thing. The

199

glass will slip in, and then it will start its work. The shards will spin and cut and gouge. You'll feel like you fell into a food processor.

"Or, you can just come on out now, and we can do away with the gratuitous violence. I'll snap your neck. You won't feel a thing."

Lindsay couldn't answer. She searched Mark's face for any sign of humanity and found none.

"No?" Mark asked. He balled his fists and struck the doorframe with a deafening blow.

Lindsay screamed.

Mark pounded the jamb again. He was trying to knock the icons loose. If even one came free, Lindsay was dead. She knew it. She knelt down and crawled across the closet floor. She reached out to hold the metal corner pieces in place. When her fingers touched the icons, a flare of fire met her fingertips. She yelped in pain and crawled away.

Mark stared in at her. A look of confusion spread across his brow. He took a step back.

"I don't understand," he said.

Lindsay gazed up. Mark looked scared, though why she didn't know. The boy next door took another step back.

Jack appeared at Mark's shoulder. His face was lined with red cuts and his black shirt was torn in a dozen places. The brand rested in his palm. Jack shot out a hand and grasped Mark by the back of the neck.

"Burn," Jack whispered, and flames exploded across the top of the metal disk. He thrust the brand forward with a punching motion, driving the searing metal into Mark's cheek.

Mark's eyes grew wide. His mouth fell open to scream, but no sound escaped. In fact, the only thing Lindsay heard was the crackling of burning skin. Lines like black veins traced over Mark's face, down his neck, and over his chest. In moments, his arms, his torso, every exposed inch of skin was marred with the black lines, like a ragged mesh.

Jack backed away. He dropped the brand and watched in awe as Mark fell to the floor. The lines blossomed into black flowers of charred skin. Mark's eyes, once as beautiful as a summer sky, turned white and cold and empty.

"Is he dead?" Lindsay asked. "Really dead this time?"

Jack looked up from Mark's charred remains. "I think so," he said, as if confirming a UFO sighting.

"I thought he couldn't die," Lindsay said.

Jack had no answer. He stood with his hands on his hips, looking like a fireplug. Slowly he shook his head back and forth. "Is it possible?" he asked.

From the back of the room, Doug Richter moaned. Jack ran to him and knelt down. The man's entire body was covered in dust. Lindsay couldn't tell how badly he was hurt, but he wasn't dead, and she was grateful for that.

"I think it's over," Jack said, helping Doug sit up. A shower of dust fell from the tall man. He shook his head and coughed, raising a cloud around himself. "He's gone."

"He can't die," Doug said, his voice a thin and pained squeak. He wiped the remnants of filth from his face. "You know that. He will always walk among us."

"But look," Jack insisted, pointing toward the closet door.

Lindsay stood up. The blackened skeleton, which was all that remained of Mark, did not move. The flesh did not re-form. He was gone. Truly gone. It was time to get away from this place and find her parents, to hug them and tell them how much she loved them.

She stepped forward. Orange light flared, and her skin erupted with pain as if someone had set it on fire. Lindsay yelped and leaped back from the doorway. She searched her blouse and body for the source of the searing ache, but neither fabric nor flesh was scorched.

"You see?" Doug said. "Always among us."

"Oh no," Jack said, his face crumbling to an expression of utter despair. "That poor, dear girl."

"What's happening?" Lindsay cried. Panic replaced her pain. It sparked throughout her entire system, making her skin tingle and twitch disturbingly. Desperate to be free, she tried again to step over the threshold, and another sheet of burning agony pressed against her body. This time her scream was piercing. She danced anxiously from foot to foot, unable to understand what was happening to her.

"Jack?" she shrieked. "What's going on?"

And for the second time that night, Lindsay felt something move low in her abdomen, like a worm twisting to make itself comfortable.

Mark?

Always among us.

203

A boy named Chris Herren wandered through the
woods, swatting at the ground and the occasional
shrub with a thick tree branch. Snow crunched
beneath his boots. A chill wind worked its way
beneath his scarf.

Get some fresh air, his father said. *You're not
going to enjoy the trip if you just sit inside*.

Yeah, like this festival of nettles and poison oak
was going to improve if he immersed himself in
it. He didn't know what the hell to do in the
woods. He knew what bears did in the woods,
which made his current trek all the more disturbing, but Chris had grown up in a co-op in Midtown
Manhattan. He didn't even like to be *close* to

nature, let alone surrounded by it. They were supposed to be skiing, but there wasn't enough snow. Oh, there was enough to make walking a chore, but not enough good powder to justify waiting in the lift line. They didn't even bother driving to the resort that morning.

He swung the tree branch, connected solidly with a fir trunk, and dropped the stick. Chris looked back down the trail the way he'd come, and then up the hill. A glimmer of light caught his eye, and he peered through the trees to get a better look. More than likely, he was seeing a bit of sunlight catching the top of a discarded beer can. But as he focused on the place from which the glint came, he noticed more movement. A slender tendril of smoke rose through a break in the trees.

A chimney? Neighbors?

Chris wondered if anyone his age lived up there. Or even better, maybe some college kids had rented a cabin for the Christmas break. Thoughts of keg parties and scantily clad coeds flitted into his mind.

It was worth a look.

The cabin, a large log structure, appeared slowly. Each step Chris took revealed another row of logs, then the break of the porch on the right. A window came into view, dark as night. Then he saw the porch railing and the rest of the window.

Chris hugged a tree, not wanting to get caught sneaking up on the place. He just wanted to see what his neighbors looked like. If they seemed cool, he'd wander up, pretending to not even notice the cabin until he was standing right next to it. The place looked empty, but he saw a car parked in the drive. Sunlight shimmered off a perfectly polished bumper. That's what had caught his eye on the trail.

To his left Chris noticed a slight rise that would put him above the cabin's foundation. He walked to it and climbed up. When he reached the top of the mound, he peered at the cabin and was shocked to see a face in the window.

She was a pretty girl, though a bit plump in the face. *Maybe she's just built a little thick,* Chris thought. He couldn't be sure, because from where he stood, he only saw her from the breasts up, which was cool. They looked nice. And she was definitely cute.

He tried to look busy, tried to look cool. He tried to look like anything but a stalker who was trying to sneak a peek into the house, but he was right out in the open on the rise. He smiled.

The girl waved at him, and Chris felt a tingle of excitement in his belly.

The family vacation is looking up, he thought.

Then another face appeared. The man was only slightly taller than the girl. His face was thick and strong-looking. Maybe he was the girl's father or husband, but Chris didn't think so. At least, he hoped not. She was about his age, and the guy looked as old as his granddad. He also looked pissed off.

The man wrapped an arm around the girl and guided her away from the window. Chris's sense of disappointment flared, then went out completely. He saw the bulge of the girl's stomach when she turned to the side.

No way, he thought. *Pregnant is so not hot.*

So Chris walked off the snowy mound. He picked up the trail where he'd left it and began the walk down.

EPILOGUE

A mournful rumbling shook the old Georgian deeply. The sound was like thunder, but last night's storm was over, and the way Shirley rolled up on her knees with her jaws stretched open made it seem as if, somehow, it had come from her.

She panted, shivered, exhaled, and grinned giddily. The moonlight picked up a patina of ghostly sweat on her face that made her pale skin glisten. She blinked a few times and noticed how the others were staring. Then she began to sob.

"I told you it was horrible," she said, collapsing forward. "That poor girl, trapped with that thing inside her."

A nonplussed Anne rolled her eyes. "Please.

That overprivileged brat got just what she deserved. She made it with a guy she barely knew without any protection. Like she didn't know about the birds and the bees?" She rolled closer to the whimpering Shirley in a predatory fashion. "But the big question is why you got all *Rainman* to try to keep from telling it."

Anne looked up and melodramatically scanned the ceiling, where flecks of fraying plaster jutted from darkness. "Hmm. No Christmas lights or angelic hordes. I'm guessing it wasn't your story. Why the fuss?"

Shirley tried to slow her breathing. "When it first came to me, I didn't know it wasn't mine. I was . . . I was just afraid it might be, I guess."

"Right," Anne said. "But that's never happened before. Did it hit too close to home? Were you maybe not a virgin when you died?"

Shirley looked nervously around. "No, I would *never*! I mean, I don't know! That's not fair! You know I don't remember! None of us do!"

Her objections were loud, bringing Daphne and Mary out of the story's haze.

"What are you on about now, Anne?" Daphne said, her brow twisted deeply in disapproval.

"You've no heart at all," Mary chimed in. "Lindsay was in love. It was tragic."

"Well, I did like her spirit, if not her taste in men," Daphne said. "She was a fighter. Thought on her feet. Guess you can't always help what the heart wants."

"Yeah," Anne said. "That's why we have laws. And agreements. Things that people can stick to when it's not in their selfish best interests. You know, like agreements about how games should be played?"

Daphne sighed loudly. "That again. How much longer are you going to drag our noses through it? We gave you your three tries and you lost. Now you're taking it out on Shirley? Can't you let anything go?"

Anne's face wrinkled. "Maybe I just can't stomach the way Shirleykins whines even when she wins. She's the only one who's never even been in the Red Room, right? What's that about?"

"Can I help it if I'm sensitive?" Shirley shot back. Then she curled into a little ball and started fidgeting with her hair again.

Daphne rose, walked over, and patted Shirley's shoulder. "The old dame probably just figures it'd drive her crazy permanently. She wants to keep us afraid and, well, Shirley's already afraid."

Shirley pulled out another strand of her hair and stared at it. "I know I'm a little jittery sometimes, but, really, I can't help the way I am, even if I'm not sure who that is exactly. After all, what if it *had* been my story? What if I'm here because I committed suicide just to avoid giving birth to a monster?"

"Oh, please. Turn the drama volume down," Anne said. "What if Mary was a serial killer or I was a nun?"

"Ha! That'd be the day," Daphne said. "But all this talk's got me thinking. Anyone ever wonder why we don't remember?"

"The shock of passing, I always supposed," Mary said wistfully. "Isn't that final breath bad enough, no matter how gentle?"

"No way," Anne said. "If that was it, this place would be full up. We'd have enough for a million spirit march."

"Maybe it's some trick of the Headmistress, a way she has to keep us all here," Daphne said. "She could be that powerful, I imagine." She rose and stretched.

"Or maybe our deaths really were particularly

terrible," Shirley added.

"Whatever. We don't have a clue. Deal with it," Anne said.

Daphne sighed. "Well, ladies, I hate to admit, but Anne was right when she said we were pushing our luck. Unless we want to risk discovery again, I'm thinking we should call it a night." She turned and looked at the raven-haired girl. "Anne, let's try to start over, okay? Since we skipped you last night, you hide the Clutch tonight. All right?"

"Fine," Anne said. *Just fine.*

She sat on her knees, put her long thin arms out on the floor, and scooped all five bones toward her. Then she took the vermilion bag, the Clutch, loosened the top, and one by one placed the bones inside. Straightening, she tightened the cord and tied a loose knot in it.

"Well?" she said, looking at the others. "You three going to gawk at me all night? I thought the idea was that only one of us knows where the bones are, so that if the others get caught, they can't tell what they don't know."

"Very well," Mary said, rising. "But where shall we gather next?"

Shirley shrugged. "We haven't been in the

kitchen in a while. I like all the pots and pans, and there's lots of exits and hiding places."

"Whatever," Anne said. "Such a little housewife."

"The kitchen will be fine," Mary said.

"Tomorrow night then, in the kitchen," Daphne said, heading off. "Don't be too long, Anne. The Headmistress will be up soon, and we wouldn't want her to find you wandering where you're not supposed to."

"Chill," Anne said, rising.

Mary's eyes wandered to the red bag in Anne's hand. It looked like a bloody wound against her black T-shirt.

"Anne," Mary began.

"Yeah?"

"Nothing. Never mind. Until tomorrow eve," she said, turning away.

With that, the three girls faded off into the cracks and corners, leaving Anne behind.

She smiled, looked around, then stuffed the bag beneath the loose floorboard she'd considered pushing the skull under with her toe. Satisfied that all the red cloth was covered by wood, she straightened her shirt and looked up and down the hall.

It was long and dark and seemed to go on for-ever. The moonlight was fading, leaving only the wavering dark.

"Mary?" Anne called in a quiet voice. "Daphne?"

There was no response. She looked up at the ceiling and eyed it wryly. "Shirleykins?"

Again, nothing.

They'd played without her and called her a monster, and they hadn't even really apologized. Not that it would've made a difference.

I'll show them who they're messing with.

With a Mona Lisa half smile, Anne walked, not east toward the dormitory, where the Headmis-tress insisted they stay, but west to the staircase, where she climbed up and up, floor after floor, until she reached the sixth. Here was the wide hall, once elegant, now crumbling, that held the thick oak door to the Headmistress's room. That was one advantage they held over her. They always knew where to find her, but at night, despite the fact that she seemed able to extend her presence anywhere in the orphanage, the Headmistress didn't always seem certain where to find them.

Anne had one more story she wanted to tell

tonight, and she didn't need the bones to do it. She raised her hand and, after pausing a moment to allow the chill of fear to pass through her, knocked on the thick wood, once, twice.

After her third rap, the door creaked, vibrating slightly as it came free from the jam. There seemed to be no one opening it, though. A blast of cold, rank air hit Anne. She dizzied, then tried to steady herself as she took a step inside.

It seemed more forest than room. More swamp than forest. There were glimpses of rot and mold. Water dripped in thick streams from the edges of the hole in the ceiling, rolling over and apparently feeding some sort of thick green slime.

Fear rose along her spine like a living thing and swelled until it filled her completely. The more she became afraid, the more she noticed a fine mist hovering in the dark.

The droplets came together, and in moments the Headmistress appeared, her gown perfect and tight as always, her skin smooth as ice, her eyes dead.

Recognizing Anne, she did not seem amused.

"Well? Have you come back for more?"

Anne managed to swallow and shake her head.

"No. I just wanted to tell you that I'm like really sorry."

The creature before her twisted its head.

Is she buying?

"I mean, I know you're just trying to take care of us, right? To . . . raise us properly? I mean, where we'd be without that, without you? Guess I forgot that."

"Yes. I suppose you did," the Headmistress said. Her lips, so thin and gray, twisted up at the corners. The net effect looked more like the twitch of a dying worm than a smile. Then the worm split long-ways in the center, showing a row of gray teeth. "But I'm so glad you remembered. Things don't have to be so hostile between us, you know, as long as you obey the rules and show the proper respect. That's what rules are for, after all. Was there anything else?"

Anne nodded. "Yeah, speaking of rules and respect. It's the others. They're . . ."

"Yes?"

"They're planning to meet tomorrow night after curfew. And I know where."

The split worm of a smile twisted wider. "Do you? Dear child, you look so tired. Let's chat a moment before the day begins."

Anne stepped deeper into the swamp of a room, gritting her teeth, clenching her hands, thinking, *The Headmistress will get them all this time, even Shirley. And I'll have the bones to myself.*

TO BE CONTINUED

ROLL THE BONES WITH

Daphne, Anne, Shirley, and Mary are trapped in an abandoned orphanage. As they "roll the bones" to determine who'll tell the evening's tale of violent death, they must also watch out for the evil spirit who is stalking them. This night, the tale told is of high school senior Mandy. Mandy and her friends are recovering from the shocking, grisly death of their classmate Nicki. Mandy's slowly putting her life back together when she realizes that Nicki's killer is coming after her.

Daphne, Anne, Shirley, and Mary are rolling the bones once again, while hiding from the evil Headmistress. Tonight's scary tale focuses on seventeen-year-old Devin, whose garage band Tom is about to hit the big time. But Devin's pleasant world is ripped apart when a deadly creature appears as though summoned by the band's new song. It violently kills first one, then another of Devin's bandmates. Who's next?